SPECIAL MESSAGE TO READERS

THE RELUCTANT STAND-IN

Kathryn Kirkwood decides to go and offer an apology to wealthy entrepreneur Sebastian Grant for being unable to prevent his wife's tragic death, and unexpectedly finds herself offering to act as temporary stand-in for his young son's departing nanny. When she discovers that Sebastian has taken over the company that her father and sister work for and is threatening redundancies, she is torn between family loyalty and her growing feelings for him and his son, Jamie. And the beautiful but haughty Cassie seems to have designs on Sebastian as well . . .

Books by Susan Udy
in the Linford Romance Library:

THE CALL OF THE PEACOCK
FORTUNE'S BRIDE
DARK FORTUNE
DANGEROUS LEGACY
REBELLIOUS HEARTS
SUSPICIOUS HEART
TENDER TAKEOVER
DARK SUSPICION
CLIFF HOUSE
THE UNFORGIVING HEART

SUSAN UDY

THE RELUCTANT STAND-IN

Complete and Unabridged

LINFORD
Leicester

First published in Great Britain in 2014

First Linford Edition
published 2015

A catalogue record for this book is available from the British Library.

ISBN 978–1–4448–2373–8

Published by
F. A. Thorpe (Publishing)
Anstey, Leicestershire

Set by Words & Graphics Ltd.
Anstey, Leicestershire
Printed and bound in Great Britain by
T. J. International Ltd., Padstow, Cornwall

This book is printed on acid-free paper

1

Kathryn Kirkwood stared at the solid oak door in front of her, wondering nervously if she was doing the right thing in coming here. Supposing he reacted in the same way that he had with Rosie — furiously? But he wouldn't, would he? It was now over two years since it had happened; it had only been a matter of six weeks or so when Rosie paid her visit.

Oh, stop being such a coward and just do it, she told herself. *What's he going to do to you? Beat you up — ?*

She jabbed at the doorbell and almost at once heard the sound of someone approaching within before the door was pulled open. And there he was: Sebastian Grant.

She knew this because he exactly matched Rosie's description: a man in his early thirties, good-looking, tall, six feet one or two, and who clearly took regular exercise judging by his physique. He had piercing blue eyes which, at this moment, were fixed firmly on her; a straight, almost Grecian nose; the sort of jawline that hinted at a man who knew what he wanted and was fully prepared to go all-out to get it; and all of this was topped by a thick mane of hair the colour of maple syrup.

'Yes?' When Kathryn didn't speak, he went on, 'Can I help you?'

His searching gaze missed nothing, she was sure, of her mahogany, shoulder-length hair, her toffee-coloured eyes, her slightly tip-tilted nose, and her full lips. He did have the decency to stop at her mouth, but she sensed that he was also taking note of her full breasts — too full in Kathryn's opinion, her smoothly rounded hips, and her legs. Legs that — again, only in her opinion — were her best feature: shapely, with slender ankles.

'Um — ' she swallowed once more. 'I-I'm Kathryn Kirkwood.'

He clearly didn't have the faintest

idea who she was. Well, why would he? They'd never met and she didn't suppose Rosie had mentioned her on that first, and only, disastrous meeting.

'Yes?' he again prompted, with more than a hint of impatience this time.

'Um — I was at the scene,' she gulped, her nervousness finally getting the better of her, 'wh-where your wife had her . . . accident.'

His gaze darkened but he didn't speak.

'I-I saw what happened. I believe my friend came to see you afterwards.' She knew very well that Rosie had called. She should do; she'd been regaled with each minute detail of the meeting. Rosie's apology had apparently been met with a furious demand as to why she hadn't done something, seeing as she'd been there at the time.

'Did you just stand there,' he'd demanded, 'and watch? Like some damned voyeur?'

Poor Rosie had stammered, 'N-no, I-we tried — ' But words had failed her and, with a muttered, 'Sorry, I shouldn't have come,' she'd turned and fled.

'Yes, if you mean — ' he hesitated and his brow creased. He massaged it with the fingers of one hand, obviously struggling to recall Rosie's name.

'Rosie, Rosie Mitton.'

'Aah, yes — of course.' Once again, he fell silent.

'I'm so sorry that we couldn't get to your wife in time.'

'From what I was told by the police, some other witnesses said no one could have. She was much too quick.'

'Well maybe, but I do feel we could have done something.'

'Like what?' he bluntly demanded.

'Well — as I said, if we could have reached her in time, we maybe could have prevented what happened. I still feel very bad about it.'

'Don't. By all accounts, my wife was determined to end her life. I doubt anyone could have stopped her.' His tone was one of bitterness now, not surprisingly. His wife had deliberately chosen to leave both him and their baby son in the worst way possible. 'I'm afraid I treated your friend rather badly, my only excuse being I was still in some sort of shock. Will you convey my apologies to her?'

'I will.'

Whether Rosie would accept the apology was debatable. In the immediate aftermath of the visit she'd been very shaken, but that had speedily changed to fury at Sebastian's insensitive attitude. 'Anyone would think I'd pushed her,' she'd ranted.

'Look, don't stand on the doorstep,' he unexpectedly said. 'Please, come in.'

She followed him into a spacious and beautifully appointed sitting room, and as she looked around her, it all came flooding back: the horror; the sensation of utter helplessness to prevent what was unfolding in front of them; the feeling of guilt that followed and still lingered to this day. She'd told herself a thousand times that if they had reacted faster, they might have been able to do something, but they'd been frozen by what it was they were witnessing. Their paralysis had only lasted for a matter of seconds, but it had delayed them long enough for the tragedy to finish playing itself out.

She and Rosie had been walking home together after viewing an apartment in the village that Kathryn had been thinking of buying, energetically arguing the pros and cons of it. Rosie thought she should go for it; Kathryn wasn't so sure. 'It's more than I planned to pay — ' she protested. 'I'm not sure I'll be able to afford the mortgage — or even if I'll get a mortgage on it.'

''course you will. You're in a well-paid job.'

'I don't know,' she said. 'It's a huge financial commitment. Maybe I should just rent somewhere.' She'd never had her own place, and at the age of twenty-four she'd decided it was more than time that she did. As much as she loved her family, she needed her independence.

But her thoughts had been stopped

right there by the sound of Rosie shouting, 'What the hell does she think she's doing?' Words which almost instantly changed into a cry of complete horror. Kathryn had turned her head and seen a woman running across the pavement, heading straight for the road and an approaching lorry.

Kathryn and Rosie had stood transfixed with horror for those few vital seconds before beginning to race towards her. They were too late. Before they or anyone else could reach her, she'd leapt in front of the lorry; and despite the heroic efforts of the driver to miss her, the vehicle had struck her, killing her instantly by the look of her crumpled body lying in the road.

Two other witnesses had confirmed their version of events. It had undoubtedly been suicide. But even now, Kathryn felt that they should have been able to prevent what had happened — if they'd just reacted straight away. The guilt had plagued her ever since, resulting in this visit. She wanted to see for herself that Sebastian Grant and his small son were all right. But most of all, she wanted to offer her own apology for her fatal lack of action.

'I'm sorry,' she now said. 'I know it's been over two years but I felt I had to come.'

He cocked his head to one side and asked, 'Yes, but why now? As you say, it's been over two years.'

'I left the village almost right afterwards — for personal reasons. I've only just returned, s-so I thought I'd call in on my way home and-and — '

'Well, you're very kind but no apology is necessary. I'm sure if there'd been anything that you could have done, you would have done it. You and your friend.'

Kathryn gnawed at her bottom lip, a habit she resorted to in times of stress. 'Well, nonetheless, I'm sorry.'

She was about to take her leave when the door to the room opened and a young woman strode in. An attractive young woman.

Kathryn felt a jolt of surprise. So, he'd found someone else. Clearly, he was fine. She'd had no need to put herself through this . . . this ordeal; he'd discovered consolation in this shapely young woman. But she swiftly discovered that she was wrong.

'I'm off now, Sebastian,' the woman said. 'Jamie's in the kitchen with Joyce.' Kathryn assumed Jamie was Sebastian's son.

'Okay. By the way, Linda, this is Kathryn Kirkwood. Kathryn, meet Linda, my son's nanny. She's leaving us, sadly, to get married.' He grinned ruefully. 'You don't know anyone looking for a job, do you? I need a new nanny — urgently.'

Linda broke in. 'Look — I really do have to go. Lots to do for the big day.'

'Of course you do. Mustn't keep Rob waiting.' Sebastian grinned and walked over to her to take her hand. 'I couldn't have managed without you, Linda. Thank you for all you've done, and the very best of luck.'

And then she was gone, in a flurry of hand-waving and even a brief kiss on Sebastian's cheek. Kathryn wondered exactly how close they'd been. That kiss, no matter how fleeting, had been unusual, surely, between an employer and his employee. And why had he left it so late to look for a replacement nanny? Linda must have warned him weeks ago that she was leaving. You didn't suddenly up sticks and decide to get married — did you?

He turned back to her again. 'I've interviewed dozens of women. I wouldn't let a single one of them look after my cat, never mind my son.'

'How old is he?'

'Four — just.'

And then — and Kathryn had no idea why she said what she did — she blurted out, 'I'll do it. I'll take care of him.'

'Why would you do that?' Sebastian looked astonished. And no wonder; it must have been the last thing he'd expected. And why would he agree? He didn't know the first thing about her.

'Well, I'd like to help and-and it would only be till you found someone else.' Kathryn smiled weakly at him. If she could have grabbed the madly impetuous words back she would have, but it was too late for that. Far too late. All she could do now was blunder on, digging herself deeper and deeper into the hole she'd made; the hole that was the direct consequence of her guilt. 'I-I suppose I'd be a sort of stand-in. I'm not currently employed, so — '

'I don't know what to say.' He was studying her through narrowed eyes. 'But, on the other hand, if you're serious?'

'I am.' What else could she say? No, sorry, I've had second thoughts? You're on your own? Hardly. 'I have to be honest, though,' she went on, hoping that this would prove to be her escape route, 'I've had no experience of minding children.'

But those hopes were speedily dashed. 'Isn't childcare instinctive in women?'

He raised a quizzical eyebrow at her.

'Um, I-I don't know. I suppose — '

He didn't let her finish, however. It was as if he were afraid that if he did she'd change her mind. 'Can you start on Monday?' It was now Friday afternoon; late afternoon.

Kathryn felt her mouth drop open. Monday, for heaven's sake? She hadn't bargained on that when she'd made her impetuous offer. She would have barely had time to set foot back in Willow Green. But apart from that, didn't he want to find out a bit more about her? This was the care of his only son they were talking about, after all.

'Well, I — ' She closed her mouth again, unable to think of a single reason not to do as he wanted. 'I suppose so.' And again, she smiled weakly.

'Um — there is just one thing more,' he went on. 'I would expect — no, need you to live in.'

2

'Live in?' Kathryn hadn't anticipated that. Mind you, that could be the perfect excuse for retracting her offer. But then something occurred to her. Doing this, living here, would mean that she wouldn't have to remain at home. She'd have a breathing space of sorts — before trying, once again, to find a place of her own.

It was what she'd been trying to do before she left the village, after all — with no success. For the truth was that over the last seven or eight years her mother had grown increasingly interfering, to the point of trying to dictate to Kathryn what she should do, how she should live her life — even, at times, what she should think. In the end it had become unbearable. Hence, Kathryn's bid for freedom by purchasing her own flat. Her failure to do that had been what had led her to leave the village almost right afterwards to work in Birmingham. She'd been very fortunate to find a job so quickly; it had been the first position she'd applied for in actual fact. But now she was on her way back, to reside once more under her mother's jurisdiction. A factor that, upon reflection, had probably subconsciously played a large part in her impetuous and ridiculous offer. Because what did she know about caring for a small child? Absolutely nothing — that's what.

'Yes,' Sebastian was saying, 'I need someone to get Jamie up and give him his breakfast. He's an early riser — which, I'm ashamed to admit, I'm not.' He grinned at her and she felt the breath catch in her throat as she asked herself what on earth was she doing, offering to work for this — this handsome man. And not just work for him, but actually share the same house with him.

Was she out of her mind?

Because the fact was that if he

grinned at her like that on a regular basis — well, she wouldn't be answerable for the consequences.

'Um, well . . . okay. But don't you want to know something about me?'

'Of course, but not now. My instincts about people tell me that you'll make a perfect carer for my son. We can talk about your CV on Monday. I really do have to go out now — an appointment I can't miss.'

She wondered who'd be looking after his son while he was gone. He must have made some sort of provision. He didn't look the sort of man to neglect a child.

'I can't thank you enough,' he went on. And that was that. Seconds later he was showing her out, and she was committed. 'I'll see you at eight o'clock on Monday then.'

She thumped her hands against the steering wheel as she headed for her parents' house. How was she going to explain all of this at home? Her mother had been horrified to hear of Sebastian's response to Rosie's apology. 'Arrogant man! Just what you'd expect from someone like him,' she'd told Kathryn on one of the occasions when she'd phoned home. Quite what she'd meant by that Kathryn had no idea. She didn't know Sebastian Grant, even though he lived in the village and had done for a while. His reputation, however, was widely gossiped about, so she guessed her mother felt as if she did know him. In fact, he'd become almost a celebrity, on a par with the likes of Alan Sugar. He'd been labelled a daring, exploitative, ruthless entrepreneur, only out to make money — and if the rumours were to be believed, with no consideration for the people that he was trampling upon in the process. It was said he'd made thousands redundant over the past few years. That must be what had influenced her mother's view of him. That and Rosie's tale of his unnecessarily cruel reception of her apology.

And then there was Matt. What was he going to think of what she was doing?

Matt Bradley and she had been an

item now for over three and a half years. They'd met when Kathryn had been twenty-two — nearly twenty-three, as had Matt, and been instantly attracted to each other. Attracted? That was an understatement. He'd quite literally swept her off her feet. He'd rushed around a street corner, straight into her. Only by dint of lifting her into his arms immediately had he prevented her from falling over.

'Oh Lord! I'm so sorry,' had been his first words to her. Then his eyes had gleamed as they took in her flushed cheeks, her parted lips, her heaving breasts. 'Look, let me buy you a drink to make up for my clumsiness.'

And that had been the start of it. Before as much as an hour had passed, she'd felt as if she'd known him all her life. She was a mere step away from falling in love — as he was also, he'd told her later. From then on, they met most evenings. But despite their closeness, not once in all their hours together had Matt mentioned marriage.

She'd hinted at it a few times, but either he hadn't understood her or he'd chosen to ignore it. Yet he'd told her regularly that he loved her, and bought her presents galore. Everything except the one thing she really wanted, that was: an engagement ring.

She sighed now. Matt was a handsome man — not as handsome as the man she'd just left, it was true. But looks weren't everything. Character was more important, and Matt had that in spades. He also had a pronounced sense of humour that she couldn't help but respond to, even though, as had happened several times, she'd been the butt of it. She was sure he hadn't meant to be cruel; he just couldn't seem to help himself.

Her heart missed several beats.

This weekend would be the first time she'd seen him since he left. His firm had transferred him to Dubai, just a month before the tragedy, in order for him to set up the IT side of a subsidiary company to the one he worked for. It had all taken a lot longer than expected.

However, his departure and her failure to find a home of her own had been just two of the reasons for Kathryn leaving Willow Green; the third, more compelling one, had been the suicide. She'd wanted to escape the appalling memory of it, as well as the recurring nightmares, and had hoped a change of scene, a challenge in the form of a new job, would help her to put it behind her. It had eventually, but it had taken several weeks.

She'd believed her and Matt's separation would only be for twelve months or so and once Matt returned, so would she. It hadn't worked out that way, however. His contract had been extended and so Kathryn had stayed away as well. She had struggled to ignore the fact that his phone calls had become more and more infrequent the longer he was away, and when he did ring her the conversations had been rushed and unsatisfactory. She couldn't recall the last time he'd told her he missed her, or that he loved her.

But now, she reassured herself, with both of them home again, things would swiftly return to normal and she was sure he'd ask her to marry him. They could then embark upon a life together, find a home, and maybe — just maybe — start a family.

Matt had been outraged when she'd phoned and told him what had happened, and how Sebastian had treated Rosie. 'The man must be mad,' he'd said. 'That, or feeling guilty. After all, if his wife was driven to commit suicide she must have been very unhappy — and that's most likely down to him.' Which was an aspect of it that Kathryn hadn't previously considered.

So, what was he going to say when she told him that she'd agreed to go and work for the madman — not merely work for him, but live in his house?

She pulled onto her parents' driveway with more than a little trepidation about the news that she had to deliver. Her mother must have been watching for her because the front door was opened the minute she pulled on the brake. Both of her parents came out to greet her, followed with a great deal more reluctance by her younger sister, eighteen-year-old Jess. She possessed all the indifference of today's teenager to anything other than her own concerns. For those things her enthusiasm, naturally, was boundless. Jess had an earpiece in and was absorbed in whatever was being played through it. She didn't give her sister more than a cursory glance.

'Hi, Jess,' Kathryn said as she was swept into her mother's arms and then her father's. Jess didn't even hear her, judging by the complete lack of any sort of response.

'Come in, darling,' Helen, her mother, urged. 'Dinner is almost ready. I've prepared your favourite — roast beef with all the trimmings. I know it's not Sunday, but . . . '

Richard, her father, winked at her and murmured, 'That means a meal large enough to feed an entire village and still have plenty left over for seconds.'

'Mum,' Kathryn moaned, 'I'm trying to keep my weight down.'

'Don't be silly, Kathryn,' her mother sternly rebuked her. 'You have absolutely no need to diet. You're to forget such rubbish. I insist.'

Here we go, thought Kathryn: her mother's first directive — the first of many, she was sure. Thank heavens she wouldn't be staying here longer than the weekend. However, she still had to clear the hurdle of telling Helen what she was about to do. Her heart missed a beat — well, several beats. Lord knew what sort of row would ensue. A pang of dread stabbed at her.

'So, you're back — finally,' Jess sharply and unexpectedly retorted.

'Oh my, she hears — and even speaks,' Kathryn jested. 'Thank you for those welcoming words, Jess. It's nice to see you too.'

'Kathryn.' Her father gently pulled her away from the others.

Kathryn turned her head and looked at him. 'What? What is it?'

'Matt phoned,' he said in a low voice. 'He can't make tonight — he'll see you, hopefully, tomorrow. He'll ring you later. He's meeting someone this evening; business, I think — he didn't go into details.'

Kathryn wondered why he hadn't rung her himself, instead of going through her father. Disappointment stabbed at her. She'd been so looking forward to being with him, talking to him, holding him, kissing him — expected that he'd be here waiting for her, eager to make plans for their future. But now it sounded as if even tomorrow was uncertain. How could he do this to her? Surely he must be feeling the same as she was — impatient to be together. He hadn't managed a single visit to England in all the time he'd been away, so in demand had he been by the company he was out there working for, apparently. And Kathryn had missed him terribly. She'd thought he felt the same way, despite his increasing coolness on the phone whenever they spoke. She'd put that down to the length of time they'd been parted. It would inevitably have some sort of effect on their relationship; she understood that. But now, that conviction was being seriously undermined as she asked herself what on earth could be more important to him than being with her on his first evening home — the woman he was supposed to love, had said he loved, more times than she could recall.

'Sorry, darling,' Richard went on. 'You must be disappointed.'

They'd reached the sitting room by this time, where her mother had a glass of sherry waiting for each of them: dry for Kathryn, sweet for herself. Her father poured himself a whisky. Jess, of course, went straight upstairs to her bedroom, now that the tedious business of greeting her older sister was over with. Within moments, the sounds of very loud music reached them all in the sitting room.

'Jess,' Richard called through the open door, 'turn it down, please. Talk about the terrible twos,' he grimaced as he swung back to his wife and daughter. 'In my opinion, the terrible teens are far, far worse.'

Helen went back into the kitchen, presumably to attend to the final preparations for dinner.

Kathryn grabbed this opportunity to speak to her father, to warn him of what she'd agreed to and, hopefully, win his support when she told her mother. 'Dad, I need to tell you something. I called in to see Sebastian Grant on the way home.'

Her hopes were instantly crushed. He stared at her in horrified shock. 'You did what? Why, for God's sake? If you're still feeling guilty, you shouldn't. You were just a witness. You didn't push his wife into the road.'

'I know, Dad, but I felt I should go. I didn't at the time because I felt it was too soon afterwards.'

'Well I hope he didn't berate you like

he did poor Rosie.'

'No. He asked me to give his apologies to Rosie, actually. He said that there'd obviously been nothing anyone could have done.'

Richard's eyebrows reached high on his forehead at this. 'Well, he's changed his tune.'

'Yes. Um, he told me his nanny is leaving. Well, has left, actually. She went while I was there.'

'Oh?' The eyebrows lifted again.

'And I've — well, I've agreed to stand in for her, just temporarily.'

'Stand in for who temporarily?'

Unseen and unheard by either of them, Helen had slipped back into the room, an irritating habit she'd spent years perfecting, and one that couldn't have happened at a worse time.

Kathryn had wanted to choose her moment to share her news with Helen, but as she'd overheard at least a part of what she'd been telling her father, Kathryn had no option now but to come clean. As a result, the words gushed from her. 'I called on Sebastian Grant on my way here to say how much I regretted what had happened to his wife, and how sorry I was that I hadn't been able to prevent what happened.'

'For heaven's sake, why?' Helen's gaze was riveted to her daughter's face. 'It happened so long ago. I hope he didn't treat you like he did poor Rosie.'

'No, and he apologised for that.'

Helen snorted disparagingly. 'I should jolly well think so. Mind you, it's taken him long enough.' Her gaze sharpened. 'So, what's this about a temporary stand-in? Stand-in for who?'

'His nanny, Linda, is leaving.'

Helen stared at her for a long moment before saying, 'Oh no — you haven't.'

'Mum, he's very nice, really.'

'Huh! Does a leopard change its spots? Not in my experience. Once a rude, arrogant man, always a rude, arrogant man.'

'He's not a leopard,' Kathryn quietly said. 'And he doesn't seem at all arrogant — or rude, come to that.'

'That's not what I've heard.' She sniffed. 'The locals don't much care for him. He usually ignores them.'

'Well, if all they do is gossip about him, I don't blame him,' Kathryn snapped. 'Anyway, that aside, I've agreed to take care of his son — just until he finds someone experienced.'

'How could you agree to do a job that's little better than that of a servant — and for such a man?' Helen burst out. 'Are you out of your mind? What a waste of your qualifications!'

'It's only temporary, I've told you.'

Helen rounded on her husband then. 'Well, don't just stand there, Richard. Do something, say something — for once in your life, back me up.'

3

'I'm doing it,' Kathryn firmly said. Someone had to stand up to her mother. Her father clearly wasn't going to, as much as she'd hoped he would.

Helen pushed the glass of sherry, which Kathryn had barely touched, into her hand. 'Have a drink. You can ring him then; tell him you've changed your mind.'

Kathryn obediently took a sip. Her mother drained her own glass and promptly poured herself another: her second, or was it her third? Had Helen always drunk this much? If she had, Kathryn didn't remember. 'I can't do that.'

'Yes, you can.'

'No. I've said I'll go and I'm not backing out. The least I can do is help him. He's been left high and dry.'

Words seemed to fail her mother

then, which was a miracle in itself. She was rarely without something to say or some sort of opinion to offer. Kathryn copied her mother's example and took another large mouthful of the sherry, hoping it would go some way to helping her through this.

'Helen, please calm down. And is another glass of sherry wise?' Richard gently remonstrated with his wife. 'You know it gives you a headache.'

'Richard,' Helen snapped, 'I need something.'

From her husband's resigned expression, he'd clearly heard this excuse before.

'There's one other thing,' Kathryn said, her heart beginning to hammer. She took another generous swig of sherry. At this rate she was going to be falling down drunk, and then what would her mother say? Both of her parents swivelled their heads to look at her. 'I-I've agreed to-to live in — at Willow Court.'

'Kathryn,' her father said, an anxious

frown now tugging at his brow, 'are you sure about this? I mean, you're going to be living in the house of a man you know nothing about.'

Kathryn nodded. 'I know. But yes, I'm sure. And, after all, he knows nothing about me either.'

'So, how long will it be for?' her mother snapped.

She shrugged. 'How long's a piece of string?'

'How ridiculous,' Helen cried. 'What sort of an answer is that? You must be mad, completely mad.'

Kathryn had never heard her mother lose her temper in such a manner before, no matter how great the provocation. Such behaviour was a sure sign of bad breeding, she'd always maintained, and something that she, Helen, would never be guilty of.

'Helen, this really isn't helping.'

'Then what would, Richard?' Helen whirled to face her husband. 'Tell me that.' Richard said nothing, only his expression and the slight shake of his head revealing his feelings of utter helplessness in the face of such anger. 'Exactly — you can't tell me, can you? I can't believe this. It means that all of my family are working for him — that-that awful man, that — axe-man.'

Richard murmured, 'You mean hatchet-man.'

'Oh, do be quiet, Richard. And-and now, my daughter — ' Her voice was rising along with her anger. ' — my daughter has actually agreed to live with him. Unbelievable!' and with both hands swinging wildly around her head, as if trying to drive away a swarm of angry bees, Helen stormed from the room and back into the kitchen, judging by the sounds of the pans being banged around.

Kathryn frowned. 'Dad, is Mum all right? It's just that I've never heard her lose it like this before. And what does she mean, all of her family working for Sebastian Grant?'

'I-I was going to tell you later. He's taken over Supreme Foods.'

'Really? When?' Supreme Foods was a large supplier of ready-made meals to restaurants, pubs and hotels. Just lately, however, it had been struggling to survive in an increasingly competitive market.

'A month ago — well, six weeks actually. It was a hostile takeover. We're expecting redundancies — it's pretty well known he's an asset-stripper. Which means Jess and I could find ourselves out of work in pretty short order. Which, I can only assume, is why your mother is so against you going to work for him and actually live in his house.'

'Why didn't you tell me this before?' she cried in exasperation. 'We've spoken on the phone regularly enough, for heaven's sake. I wouldn't have offered to go to Willow Court if I'd known. Is that all that's wrong with Mum? Only — well, she's almost hysterical. I know she can be a bit bossy . . . ' Huh! That was an understatement if ever she'd made one.

'But this . . . well, ranting — it's simply not like her.'

Richard shook his head. 'I don't know what's wrong, but maybe it is that. Although it seems a bit more than just worry over mine and Jess's jobs. When it first happened she was annoyed, naturally, but she didn't react like this. Now, for the past three or four weeks, no one can say anything without getting their heads bitten off, especially me. Maybe it took a little while for the facts to sink in.'

'Have you asked her what's wrong?'

'No.'

'Why not?'

'Because your mother's always been a law unto herself, as you know. And I don't want to pry into something that she might not want me to know. She'll tell me when she's ready. I know I exasperate her; I always have. She gets very impatient with what she sees as my lack of any real ambition, as she puts it. If she had her way, I'd be MD of Supreme Foods by now, instead of a mere departmental manager.' He gave a wry smile. 'But it's more than that. It's as if she can't bear to look at me, or even speak to me sometimes. She won't let me touch her.' His shoulders slumped as he said this, and a look of unutterable misery suffused his face. 'And she-she goes out a lot more than she's ever done, and then refuses to tell me where she's been, other than that she's been walking.'

Kathryn went to him and wrapped her arms around him. She couldn't believe what she was hearing. Her mother walking? She hated walking. She didn't even own a pair of walking shoes. Something was very wrong. For all her faults, Helen had never been this extreme. Oh no. A notion she would never have previously considered if her father hadn't just said what he had, sprung into Kathryn's head.

Could her mother be having an affair?

As unthinkable as that was, it was the only explanation she could come up with, which could mean that it was guilt that was making her behave in such an extreme manner. Guilt could make one do all sorts of crazy things, as she had discovered over the past hour or so. Did her father suspect this? Was that why he looked so crushed, so miserable? Why he didn't want to ask questions, questions that he might not want to hear the answer to? Should she ask him? No, no, she couldn't. Not without something more substantial than mere supposition to go on.

'And that's not all,' Richard went on in a low voice. 'There's trouble at work, and I don't mean the threat of redundancies that's hanging over us all.'

Kathryn pulled back, the better to see his face. 'What? What is it?'

'Food's been going missing on a fairly regular basis, mainly from my department.'

'Being stolen, do you mean?'

He nodded.

'But who by?'

'We don't know. Top brass are

reluctant to call in the police as yet. So far, it's only been modest amounts. They think it might be a member of staff, or even a couple, somehow smuggling it out. We're trying to sort it out internally — you know, unscheduled checks as people leave at the end of the day, that sort of thing. But there's a bad atmosphere. Everyone's a suspect.'

'They surely don't suspect you?'

Richard shrugged.

Kathryn stared at him. This couldn't be happening — not to her father. Anyone more honest would be almost impossible to find. No wonder he was looking so worn down. Between the problem with her mother and the thefts . . . She tried to offer some sort of comfort or reassurance. 'Oh Dad, it will all be sorted out, you'll see.'

'I hope so, because I can't continue like this, I really can't.' He lowered his face into hands that were visibly trembling, looking for all the world like a man at the end of his tether. But he hadn't answered her question — not really, not apart from his shrug — as to whether he was a suspect or not.

A sense of deep unease filled Kathryn then. How could she leave him when he seemed to need her so badly? Leave him, moreover, so that she could work for the man who was threatening his very livelihood? She was beginning to feel like a traitor. But she hadn't known any of this was happening. If she had . . .

She and her father had always been especially close, right from her early childhood. He was the one who'd put her to bed each night, read her stories, never minded repeating them as many times as she'd wanted. He'd tucked her in and kissed her. As she grew, he took her on long walks, patiently teaching her the names of the birds they saw, the wild flowers, the trees. To her mother's disgust, they even went fishing now and again — 'Little girls don't fish,' she'd angrily told them — and on one memorable occasion they'd even camped out, just for one night. There'd been a thunderstorm, she recalled, with torrential rain. Their tent had leaked — she smiled now, seeing again the empty baked bean can which Richard had strategically positioned to catch the drops. He'd always been there for her, and now here she was, abandoning him to his troubles — at least, that was what it felt like.

Not surprisingly, dinner proved a subdued affair. No one spoke very much. If it hadn't been for Jess it would have been completely silent. Kathryn told Jess what she'd told her parents but her younger sister showed no emotion at all at the news. Helen did eventually ask in an extremely cold tone, 'When are you moving in with him then?'

'Monday.'

* * *

Matt, in fact, just like Jess, showed very little emotion when Kathryn told him what she was going to be doing. They'd met for lunch the following day but, like their phone calls, it proved a very brief and unsatisfactory affair. He didn't behave at all like a man who loved her and had missed her. In fact, he was disturbingly cool towards her which, not unexpectedly, left Kathryn suspecting that their relationship was coming to an end. Strangely, that didn't produce the sort of unhappiness that she would have expected to feel, which led her to question the strength of her own feelings for him. The truth was that Matt was no longer the man she'd fallen in love with. He was subdued, with none of the wise-cracking humour she'd come to expect from him. Being away for so long had profoundly changed him; that was more than evident. They eventually parted without making any definite arrangements for meeting up again. All Matt said was, 'I'll ring you.'

She mutely added, 'Sometime, maybe.'

* * *

The weekend passed swiftly and Monday morning arrived all too soon for Kathryn, along with a feeling of dread at what she had so recklessly agreed to. Even so, she couldn't bring herself to do as her mother had commanded and retract her offer. She hadn't bothered unpacking her cases, so it was a matter of minutes to load her car ready for her departure to Willow Court. All she had to do was say a temporary goodbye to her family and head off. She wasn't going to be far away, after all, she kept reminding herself. She could return home at any time. Richard and Jess were also leaving the house. Jess worked in Richard's department at Supreme Foods, so they invariably travelled in together; Jess was involved in the preparation of the food, rather than being on the managerial side of things.

Kathryn kissed her mother goodbye. Helen remained stiff and unyielding, the disapproval radiating from her. It had made for a very uncomfortable weekend.

As Kathryn drove away, she was frowning. The relentless disapproval was bad enough — she'd expected that. But the fact that her mother hadn't even dressed to see her off — something that would have been unheard of previously — was even more worrying. Helen wouldn't normally have dreamt of stepping outside the house in a dressing gown, even onto her own driveway. Yet this morning she had done just that.

Kathryn drove slowly towards Willow Court and nervously approached the iron gates. They were standing open just as they'd been on Friday. She drove between them and crawled along the winding, tree-lined driveway. The house loomed into view and she took in what she hadn't on her first visit, as she'd been far too apprehensive about the forthcoming encounter to spend time looking about her.

She now saw a two-storey house with vertical rows of small-paned sash windows and a wonderful pediment over the front door. She gazed at a steeply sloping grey slate roof and creamy walls up which an exuberant wisteria rampaged. It was the sort of house that featured in Jane Austen novels, the sort of house she'd always dreamed of living in — just not in the capacity of a stand-in nanny.

As she pulled to a crunching halt on the wide sweep of gravel before the building, the front door opened and Sebastian Grant stood there, a small boy hopping up and down at his side. The boy — Jamie, presumably — ran down the shallow flight of steps to greet her. Sebastian didn't move.

'I'm Jamie,' he wasted no time in telling her. His smile lit up a face that was a miniature version of his father's. He held out a small hand which Kathryn instantly bent down and took.

'Hello, Jamie. I'm Kathryn.'

'I know,' he proudly told her. 'Daddy told me all about you. You're going to do what Linda did and look after me.' Kathryn saw the sheen of tears as he mentioned his previous nanny. He quickly recovered himself, though, and was soon smiling once more.

A swelling of pity for the little boy swept over her then and Kathryn did what she'd been longing to do for the past couple of moments: she let go of his hand and put her arms around him. He smelt of soap and baby talc. She hugged him close, letting his silky blond curls caress her face as he slid his arms about her neck and held on tightly.

Kathryn's heart squeezed painfully, and she vowed there and then to do her very best for this small boy for as long as she stayed with him.

He pulled away and took one of her hands again. 'Come along. I'll take you in,' he told her in an engagingly quaint manner. 'Daddy, she's coming in.'

Sebastian's mouth quirked as he struggled to hide his tender amusement. 'That's good. I was hoping she would.' His gaze met Kathryn's. 'Welcome, Kathryn.' And he, too, held out a hand. 'You go in with Jamie. I'll bring your things. Are they in the boot?'

Kathryn nodded. Sebastian Grant carrying her luggage? With all the money he was clearly making? By the look of this house — she swept another glance around — she'd have expected a legion of servants to come out and do that.

So it was Jamie who led her into the house, straight into a large black-and-white tiled hallway, from which a gracefully curving staircase swept up towards a galleried landing. Several doors led off the hall; a sizable circular table stood in the centre of this, upon which a large bowl of white lilies sat, their perfume scenting the space. The walls were panelled in light oak; antique furniture sat all around, some pieces very, very old by the look of them. Oil paintings, one or two of them looking like they were by old masters, decorated the panelled walls.

Again, she decided he'd done exceedingly well with his buyouts and takeovers, and a pang of indignation pierced her. While he was sitting extremely comfortably — luxuriously, even — her father and his fellow employees, as well as her sister, were all in fear for their jobs. Was that right or fair? She didn't think so. And yet here she was, working for him. Maybe her mother had a point, after all?

Sebastian followed them in with her various bags and suitcase. 'Shall I take some of those?' she asked. She was quite capable of carrying her own luggage, and he did look somewhat overburdened.

'No, I'm fine,' he assured her, revealing only a slight breathlessness. 'Jamie, you take Kathryn into the library while I take the bags upstairs.'

'Oh, Mr Grant, let me help you.'

Just as Kathryn had surmised, he did indeed have domestic help, in the guise of a small, plump woman wearing a spotless apron over a dark skirt and white blouse. She hastened across to him.

'Thank you, but I can manage,

Joyce,' he told her. 'Perhaps you'd like to make us some coffee. We'll take it in the library. This is Joyce Jones, Kathryn — my treasured housekeeper. I don't know what I'd do without her.'

'Oh, really now.' Despite Joyce's murmured show of modesty, she was patently gratified to be so described. So much so, that Kathryn wouldn't have been at all surprised if she'd curtseyed to her employer.

'It's true, Joyce. Daddy told me so.'

'Oh, Jamie, that's nice of you to say so.' She patted the little boy's head. 'Now you take Kathryn into the library, my duck, and I'll go make a drink. Would you like tea or coffee?' she asked, as she looked directly at Kathryn for the very first time. Warmth shone from her face and eyes. 'And may I welcome you to Willow Court.'

'Thank you. Would you mind if I called you Joyce too?'

The housekeeper beamed. 'Of course not. We don't stand on ceremony here.'

'Thank you, Joyce, and I'd love a cup

of coffee. I have to say, Jamie's already done a lot to make me feel at home.' She smiled down at the small boy, only just four years old but already a little man. A stirring of love began within her. He was gorgeous, but — a small voice of warning sounded within her — she mustn't let herself grow too attached to him or it would be very hard to leave once Sebastian found a full-time nanny.

4

In no time at all, Sebastian was striding into the library; this too was panelled, but the panelling in here was painted the colour of clotted cream, presenting a welcome contrast to the more sombre colours of the hallway. The room clearly doubled as his study because there was a huge desk covered in papers sitting to one side of an open fireplace. It being June, there was, of course, no fire. Instead, a large pot of flowers sat there, providing a vivid display of colour: pale lemon gerberas, crimson and pink Sweet Williams, white rose, and mauve and cream scented stock. Tall French doors stood open, leading directly onto a paved terrace, and from which a short flight of shallow steps led down to a vast expanse of manicured lawn. The whole room was bathed in sunshine.

Kathryn was already seated in one of

the leather button-backed chairs. Sebastian took the chair opposite. Jamie sat at Kathryn's feet, showing her one of his picture books. There was a good selection to choose from, a couple of shelves being devoted entirely to children's books and games. It was clear from that that the little boy spent a good deal of time in here with his father. The remaining shelves, reaching almost to the ceiling, were also filled with books, some of them so old they had leather bindings that were cracked and peeling; there were also many modern novels and biographies. She spotted several by Wilbur Smith and Robert Harris, as well as many other authors she hadn't heard of, and what looked like the complete set of Charles Dickens, plus several other classics. There was a flat-screen television and digital box in the room, as well as a CD player.

Joyce came in bearing a tray upon which sat a pot of coffee, along with everything to go with it. She set it down on the low table that was positioned halfway between the armchairs before leaving the room again. Whereupon, surprising Kathryn for a second time, Sebastian leaned forward and poured for both of them. 'Help yourself to cream and sugar,' he then invited.

Once she'd done that, he went on, with business-like authority, 'Right, here's how things work.'

And with that, Kathryn was made all too aware of her exact position in the household. This man was her boss, and she was his employee. Temporarily or not, that was the way things were.

'Jamie gets up at any time between six and seven o'clock. He likes his breakfast before he gets dressed, so maybe you could see to that.'

'I like a boiled egg and soldiers,' Jamie told her in the exact same tone as his father.

This time it was Kathryn who was compelled to hide her amusement. The small boy clearly spent a lot of time studying and listening to his father.

'He has his lunch at twelve, which Joyce makes, and tea at five thirty. Maybe you could see to that as Joyce will be busy preparing dinner. Bedtime is — or should be — at six o'clock.'

'I like a story then,' Jamie again chipped in.

'So that's it, really. It's up to the two of you what you do with yourselves the rest of the time.' As he finished speaking, Sebastian relaxed back into his chair and stretched his legs out in front of him to cross his ankles and steeple his fingers beneath his chin. He then proceeded to study Kathryn at some length and in silence. Finally, and just as she was beginning to feel uncomfortable beneath this scrutiny, he said, 'So, as you wanted to tell me on Friday, what was your last job? I assume it wasn't child care.' And he proceeded to smile at her, his particular brand of mind-blowing charm on view once again.

Kathryn, somehow managing to regain her composure, said, 'I was PA to the MD of an engineering company, Perkins Ltd. of Birmingham. Before that I was a secretary.'

'I know the MD of Perkins, Bob Mitchell. If he employed you to work so closely with him, you must be good — exceptional, in fact.' He stared at her once more, his expression now a reflective one. 'Um, I'm wondering . . . I'm in need of a PA as well as a nanny. My last one left somewhat unexpectedly a couple of weeks ago — family problems. What I'm thinking is, well . . . ' He grinned at her, thereby setting her pulses throbbing. 'We may as well be frank. Looking after Jamie isn't going to be particularly onerous — not for someone of your undoubted abilities. And Joyce loves to have him with her. So-o, how would you feel about working with me on a part-time basis?'

'As your PA, do you mean?'

He nodded.

'Well, I hadn't — um — ' She couldn't help wondering what her mother would have to say about that. It was bad enough that she was acting as Jamie's nanny, but to be actually involved in Sebastian's business, knowing what had happened and could still happen at Supreme Foods — all at his behest — was another matter altogether.

In the face of her stunned silence, he went on, 'For several years now I've bought failing businesses with a view to turning them round. If I'm successful, I either carry on running them or sell, whichever seems the most appropriate at the time.'

'I-I see. We-ell — ' By 'appropriate' she assumed he meant profitable.

'You'd be really helping me out.'

'What would you want me to do, exactly?'

'Computer work, mainly. Occasionally tasks concerning my personal affairs, answering the phone when I'm out, that kind of thing; organising my diary. Arranging and accompanying me on business trips. If you agree, I'll pay you — ' And he mentioned a figure that had Kathryn gasping. 'I have another room that I use as an office as well as this one. You could use that.'

'Um — ' Good grief, was that all she could say — 'um'? But the fact was, Kathryn hadn't expected to be paid. She hadn't actually thought that far ahead. She'd considered what she was about to do as nothing more than a favour to him, just till he found someone else to take over the care of his son. But his offer of the PA's job was making it all sound a bit permanent. Maybe it was time to clarify the situation — emphasize that she was here on a purely temporary basis, and that applied to both jobs.

'Well, think about it and let me know,' he went on before she could make any attempt to set the situation right. 'Your evenings are your own, naturally. I don't go out a lot and Joyce is usually here anyway. You can have Saturday afternoons to yourself as well as Sunday — all day. I presume your family live locally.'

Kathryn nodded, while wondering if he realised that half of her family plus her now — well, for the time being, at least — worked for him. 'Are you advertising the nanny's position?'

'Not me personally, no. I'm using an agency. They vet all the applicants first — and the problem is, they've no one suitable on their books at the present time.' He stood up then, bringing to an abrupt end that particular line of conversation and leaving Kathryn still not knowing how long she'd be staying. 'I'll show you your room and Jamie's. Then Jamie and Joyce can show you the rest of the house. I have some business I simply must attend to.'

With Jamie eagerly chattering at her side and still clinging to her hand, Kathryn followed Sebastian up the stairs. The small boy obviously wanted — maybe even needed — a younger woman in his life, someone like his mother. Joyce was there, it was true, but she looked to be in her mid- to late forties, and therefore was more of a grandmother figure. Once again, a stab of anguish for him went through Kathryn, making her resolve to do all she could, in the brief time she'd be here, to try and fill that gap.

The room that Sebastian waved her into took her breath away. He must have made a mistake. This couldn't be the nanny's room. It was luxurious to a ridiculous degree — five star luxury in fact, with its heavy silk curtains flanking long, not quite floor length windows, its four-poster bed, its sweep of wardrobes complete with built-in dressing table — obviously all recently fitted, but in a style that was perfectly in keeping with the period of the house. What she guessed were antique carpets covered the floor. There was even a fireplace before which were grouped an armchair and a two-seater settee. A bookcase sat to one side of the fireplace, filled with books, naturally; she noted a couple of her favourite writers. On the other side was an alcove fitted out with a television and digital box, and once again a CD player, along with a selection of discs to play.

'Um — this seems very luxurious for the nanny.'

'Oh — ' He raised an eyebrow at her. ' — this isn't the room that Linda occupied; that's further along. This is one of the guest rooms. There's an en-suite bathroom through there.' He indicated a door so well concealed she wouldn't have noticed it if he hadn't pointed it out. 'You aren't Jamie's nanny, after all. You're a guest who's helping me out for the moment — Isn't that right?' His look was a piercing one; interrogative, even.

'Well — yes, I suppose so.' She sounded doubtful, even to herself, because you didn't pay a guest to look after your child, did you?

'So, is it okay?' He tilted his head to one side as he regarded her. 'If you're not happy . . . ?'

'Oh, my goodness — I am, yes, completely. It's positively splendid,' she gushed. 'Far more luxurious than anything I've been accustomed to.'

'Good. Maybe it will tempt you to stay for a while in that case.' And he smiled at her, the warmly engaging smile that she was becoming familiar with; the one that completely changed his face, softening the ordinarily somewhat harsh features, and invariably set her heart aflutter.

'Oh, well . . . ' she began to demur. She was about to tell him that she had no intention of staying any longer than it took him to find her replacement, both for the nanny's position and the PA's, but he didn't let her finish. She was beginning to suspect he knew only too well what she wanted to say and was making sure she wasn't able to.

'Right, now for Jamie's room. Jamie, lead the way, my boy.'

Jamie, who had remained silent throughout all of this, said, somewhat self-importantly now at the task his father had set him, 'This way, please.'

Kathryn smiled as she followed him

into a bedroom two doors along that would surely be every child's dream — its enormous space was filled with all that a boy could desire. There were games plentiful and varied enough to stock the average shop, toys galore, a beautiful rocking horse, even a train set laid out in one corner.

'Well, I'll leave you to it,' Sebastian said. 'Jamie will give you a guided tour of the rest of the house. Call Joyce if you need anything.' And he leant over his son, dropping a kiss on the top of his head. 'See you both later.'

'Yes, Daddy.' Jamie seemed completely unconcerned by his father's imminent departure, saying eagerly to Kathryn, 'Do you want to have a go on my train set?'

With a fond smile at his son, Sebastian said, 'Enjoy yourselves,' and he was gone.

They spent the morning together, Jamie happily, and in great detail, demonstrating each of his toys and what it did. So much so, they had no time to explore the rest of the house. Eventually, they joined Joyce for lunch in a kitchen that could have come straight from the pages of a glossy magazine, with every gadget and labour-saving device known to man — or woman. It wasn't until that evening that Kathryn saw Sebastian again. She went downstairs after settling Jamie down for the night, expecting to eat in the kitchen with Joyce. But Joyce said, 'Oh no, Sebastian is expecting you to eat with him. He's in the library. He said would you join him there for a pre-dinner drink?'

Kathryn's feelings of surprise mixed in equal quantities with alarm must have transferred themselves to her face, because Joyce laughed and said, 'Now, don't look like that. He won't eat you — I've prepared enough food to make sure of that.' And she chuckled to herself.

'But — did Linda eat with him?'

'Oh no. But you aren't really Jamie's nanny, are you?'

'Well, no, but . . . '

Joyce laughed, even more heartily this time. 'Sebastian might seem a bit . . . well, intimidating at first. But once you get to know him, he's a lovely man. A real teddy bear.'

Kathryn thought that, as genial as he was turning out to be, a teddy bear was the last thing she would liken Sebastian Grant to. However, seeing that she had no option but to do as he'd asked, she gathered up her courage and walked from the kitchen, heading for the library. What on earth would they find to talk about? His work? The fact that both her father and sister worked for him and were in danger of losing their jobs? Should she mention that?

Even more nervous now in the wake of these thoughts than she'd been before, she entered the library to find Sebastian, glass in hand, standing before the fireplace, his brow drawn down, his expression one of brooding contemplation.

Kathryn swallowed convulsively. That

didn't bode well; he looked displeased about something. Something that she'd done — or worse, not done? But she needn't have worried, for the second he glanced up and saw her, his expression changed to one of smiling amiability.

'Hello,' he greeted her. 'How's the first day been? I hope my son hasn't worn you out. He can be a bit energetic, not to say downright boisterous.'

'Oh no, no; we've had a great time. He's shown me how every toy he possesses works, so I'm now an expert on trains and racing cars.' She began to tick each game off on her fingers. 'Not to mention Ludo, Snakes and Ladders and Snap. He's a lovely little boy, a real credit to you.'

'Thank you.' He looked genuinely gratified at her praise. 'Well, after all of that, I think you deserve a drink. What can I get you?'

Conversation after that, just as she'd feared, proved stilted. Why on earth had he invited her to join him? They had nothing to talk about other than Jamie, of course; but with that topic exhausted, she belatedly wondered if he was lonely. As much as he visibly loved his son, Jamie was too young to hold a proper conversation.

However, once they were seated at one end of a dining table that would comfortably seat twenty or so people, things grew slightly easier, whether as a result of the wine that they'd both drunk — although she'd only had a small glassful — Kathryn couldn't have said; but whatever the reason, the relaxing of the tension between them came as a welcome relief. Their talk was pretty general to start with, but then completely out of the blue he asked, 'So, do you want to act as my part-time PA?'

As his eyes glittered at her over the rim of his wine glass, she realised he was actually very keen for her to do it.

Oh heck, she decided, why not? As the day had progressed, and as much as she'd enjoyed spending time with

Jamie, she'd begun to doubt whether simply caring for him would be enough to occupy her fully on a day-to-day basis, even for just a week or two. She needed a challenge of some sort. 'Yes, I don't mind helping you out, but you really don't need to pay me so much. In fact, you don't need to pay me at all.'

'Oh, yes I do. If you're doing two jobs, which you will be — caring for Jamie and tending to my needs . . . ' He paused, quite deliberately it seemed to Kathryn. So much so that she found herself wondering what, precisely, he meant by that. Tending to his needs? Which needs would they be, then?

Her heart began to thud, which she had an uncomfortable suspicion he knew. As if to bear this out, a smile flirted almost sensually with the corners of his mouth. Her heart did a flip this time; in fact, it felt as if were turning completely over. Oh God! He knew exactly how attractive he was and, she suspected, wasn't averse to using that benefit for his own ends. In this instance, keeping her around to look after both his son and himself.

' . . . then you should be adequately recompensed,' he finished.

'Well . . . ' It didn't feel right to take money for doing what was, after all, no more than a favour.

'Fine, so be ready to start tomorrow.'

'Okay, if-if Joyce doesn't mind looking after Jamie.'

'You're kidding. She loves nothing more.'

Kathryn nervously watched him as he cut into his sirloin steak. Maybe now was the time to tell him about her father and sister working for him at Supreme Foods. She'd feel as if she were here under false pretences if she didn't. She took a deep breath and said, 'I don't know if you're aware of it, but my father and sister also work for you.'

He glanced at her in surprise, his fork poised halfway to his mouth. 'Do they?'

'Yes. My father, Richard, is manager of a department.'

'Not in the company where we have

the theft problem, I hope — Supreme Foods?' His tone was a critical one all of a sudden.

'Well, yes.'

'And your sister — where does she work?'

'She's involved in the preparation of the food.'

'Same department?' His gaze narrowed at her as he abruptly replaced his fork onto his plate, the steak largely uneaten.

'Yes, actually.' She hesitated. His expression now was one of suspicion. 'I hope you're not suggesting — ' Her words of indignation tailed off beneath the intensity of his stare.

'Please, don't stop there. Suggesting what?'

He continued to watch her from beneath heavy eyelids. She started to fidget in her seat, devoutly wishing she hadn't opened her mouth.

'Th-that either of them is involved in any way in those thefts.'

'Of course not.'

Somehow, she didn't believe him. That had come out altogether too quickly, too smoothly. She slanted a glance at him. 'Because I can assure you my father is as honest as the day.'

'Good. And your sister? What's her name, by the way?'

'Jess. And well, Jess can be . . . moody, even wilful, but she'd never do anything dishonest.'

'How old is she?'

'What's that to do with anything?'

This was fast turning into an inquisition. His gaze had hardened as he waited for her answer. In fact, he'd reverted to the harsh-featured and unapproachable man who'd initially opened the front door to her. 'Eighteen,' she said. 'Eight years younger than me.'

'Hmmm.' Even though he couldn't have helped but detect her annoyance, he made no further comment other than, 'I believe management — i.e. your father — is looking into the matter. I'm going along tomorrow to assess what's being done and how much progress is being made. I won't tolerate stealing from the company and if we discover that it is a member of staff responsible, they will be dismissed with immediate effect, whoever it should turn out to be.'

Kathryn couldn't help herself. 'And then, doubtless, you'll carry on and decide who else is leaving and who's staying.' The second the words were out, but she could have bitten her tongue off for saying them.

'What, precisely, does that comment mean?' His voice had become as hard as his eyes.

She swallowed nervously. If he acted in the same determined manner as he spoke, what hope was there for jobs at the company? Her father was clearly right to be concerned. 'Well, I'd heard you were looking to make redundancies.'

'And where did you hear that?'

'M-my father mentioned the possibility.' She nibbled at her bottom lip. Oh God! Why couldn't she keep her mouth shut? Her rashness must be the direct result of the wine she'd drunk — although such a small amount didn't normally go to her head so quickly. She poured herself a glass of water, only to glance back and encounter a gaze that still bore a marked resemblance to a mountain glacier.

'I see,' was all he said to that.

The cold anger that she'd expected in the wake of her rash remarks hadn't materialised. Still, she was left with an uneasy feeling in the pit of her stomach, making her question whether she'd made a terrible mistake in agreeing to come to Willow Court.

'I haven't made any decisions about that yet,' he went on. 'I always wait a while after taking over a business. It allows time for things to settle, to shake down. And then I find, more often than not, that redundancies aren't necessary. Of course, sometimes they are.'

'And then you ruthlessly wield the axe?'

She closed her eyes in despair. She'd

probably just guaranteed immediate dismissal for both her father and sister. They'd never forgive her or Sebastian. And as for what her mother would say — well, that didn't bear thinking about.

5

When she opened her eyes again, she noticed that Sebastian's gaze was still cool as well as impenetrable. He was leaning back in his chair as he silently considered her and what she'd said; his long fingers toyed with the stem of his wine glass. When he finally spoke, his tone, as she supposed she should have expected, given his deadpan expression, was one of complete impartiality. She had no idea what he was thinking. He could have been about to sack her as well as her father and sister. In fact, the way she was feeling at that moment, she would have welcomed such an outcome, if it ensured the employment of her family.

'No, I don't wield the axe, as you put it. First of all, I offer voluntary redundancies. Then, if that doesn't achieve the savings I'm looking for, I put people who are willing, such as the older work staff, on a part-time contract. Only in very extreme circumstances do I force redundancies upon people. Does that alleviate your concerns?'

She nodded. Words were beyond her at that point. Which, she conceded, was a blessing. She'd said more than enough already.

'And you needn't worry about your father's job,' he smoothly went on. 'I'm not planning any management redundancies. I need their expertise — so sacking them, any of them, would be very short-sighted on my part. Your sister, however . . . ' He shrugged. 'Depending on how long she's worked for the company and if I need to go to such lengths, well . . . '

'Last in, first out, you mean.'

'Something like that. It's the way of the modern world, I'm afraid, Kathryn. It's better to get rid of the few to save the majority. Surely even you would agree with that?'

'I suppose so, yes,' she grudgingly admitted.

'Good. Now, if you would excuse me — ' He got to his feet. ' — I have someone I have to see.'

'Do you still want me to act as your part-time PA and Jamie's nanny?'

He looked surprised. 'Of course, I do. Why wouldn't I?'

'Well, I thought — '

'You thought because you spoke your mind I'd dismiss you? You really think I'm that petty?' His piercing stare dared her to say yes.

'N-no, but — '

'Kathryn, there's one thing you need to know about me. I appreciate people speaking their minds. What I hate and detest are the ones who smile to your face and say one thing, then turn around once you've gone and say the exact opposite. Clearly, you have your reasons to believe I'm a heartless asset-stripper who deprives people of their jobs at a stroke.'

'No, I — '

He held up a hand. 'That's okay, you have a right to your opinion. But now that I've explained, in part, the way I work, I hope that you've changed your mind. I don't carry anyone, but if they work hard and efficiently, they have no need to worry. Okay?'

She nodded.

'Good.' He smiled with what looked like genuine warmth. It was starting to look as if he possessed all the properties of a chameleon; he had the identical ability to change colour — or mood, rather, in Sebastian's case — at the drop of a hat.

Kathryn breathed a tiny sigh of relief.

For now, at least, her father's and sister's jobs seemed secure, but she really would have to watch what she said — despite his assertion that he liked people to tell him what they thought. There would only be so much, surely, that he'd be willing to hear and not take some sort of retaliatory action over.

'So I'll see you at about ten in the morning. Does that suit you? You can help me out till about three and then return to Jamie. If you could manage to do that two or three times a week, it would be perfect.'

'Is that all?' she asked. With what he had agreed to pay her, she'd expected the PA's job to be a pretty well full-time one.

'Yes. I want Jamie to be your primary concern. He needs a younger woman's company and guidance . . . ' His words tailed off and Kathryn felt her heart swell with sympathy for him. She sensed what he'd been about to say — like Sara, his wife, would have been. However, his expression remained shuttered as he stood up, so once again Kathryn had no chance of guessing his thoughts, much as she would have liked to. 'Finish your meal.' And with that, he abruptly left the table and her and headed for the door.

'But what about yours?' she called after him. He'd left a good half of his steak uneaten, along with most of his glass of wine.

'I'm not hungry.'

* * *

She finished her meal — well, most of it, as their argument had diminished her appetite too — and left the room. She'd just reached her bedroom after helping Joyce clear up when her mobile phone rang. It was Rosie.

'Hey, how are you?' the lilting tones asked. 'Glad to be home?'

'Ye-es.'

'You don't sound very sure. What's wrong? Matt's back so you should be on cloud nine.'

'I should be, yes.'

'So why aren't you?'

'I don't want to go into it all on the phone. Shall we meet — if you're free, that is?'

'I'm free,' Rosie trilled, 'free as a bird. I did have a date but he's cancelled. Flippin' men,' she grumbled; it was an unwelcome reminder of Sebastian's equally speedy change of mood a little while ago. 'You just can't rely on 'em. I've all but abandoned any hope of finding someone prepared to commit himself to any sort of long-term relationship, so I'm trying to resign myself to lonely spinsterhood.'

'Don't be stupid. You, a spinster? Men love you,' Kathryn put in.

'Yeah, but not enough to stay with me. So how about meeting at the the Red Lion in, say, an hour?'

Kathryn checked her watch. It was just gone seven fifteen and Sebastian had said her evenings were her own. She'd have to change but she could be at the pub by eight fifteen. She'd need to get hold of a door key, though. 'That would be great. It seems ages since we had a really good chat.'

'A whole month, actually. The last time I phoned you.'

'Oh God, I'm sorry. I kept meaning to ring you back but the time just went by.'

'Yeah, yeah, excuses, excuses. Don't want to hear them. So, meet in an hour?'

* * *

It was actually eight thirty by the time Kathryn finally walked into the Red Lion. She'd had a shower and swapped the clothes she'd worn all day for something more casual, and then Joyce had had to search for a key to give her. 'I'm surprised Sebastian hasn't given you one,' she'd said.

'He probably forgot.' Or, much more likely, he wanted to wait and see how things worked out between them before entrusting her with a key to his house. Had she been premature in asking for one? But how would she get back in without a key? Joyce could well have gone to bed.

Anyway, eventually she was about to leave when she heard Jamie calling her. She went to his room to find him sitting up in bed, rubbing his eyes and very distressed. He'd obviously been to sleep and had woken again.

'I've wet the bed, Kathryn,' he tearfully told her.

'Oh, darling,' she'd said, lifting him off the damp sheet. 'Don't worry, we'll soon have that put right.'

She'd then had to go off in search of clean bed linen, after which he'd wanted another story. So in the end she'd had to rush from the house to get to the pub, and even then she was late.

Not surprisingly, Rosie was already there, two glasses of white wine on the table in front of her. One — her own — was practically empty. She pushed the other towards Kathryn. 'I was just wondering if you'd changed your mind. What took you so long? You live nearer than I do, for heaven's sake.'

'Not anymore,' Kathryn said, lifting her glass to her lips and taking a gulp in preparation for what she had to tell her friend. Because she suspected that Rosie wouldn't be any more pleased with what she was doing than her parents had been.

'What do you mean? Have you moved? Found a flat? God! That was quick. You've only just got back.'

Kathryn paused and regarded her friend. They'd been friends since junior school; in fact, Rosie was her closest friend. Rosie was also everything that Kathryn wanted to be — pretty, bubbly, slender, her weight never varying no matter what she ate; whereas Kathryn only had to glance at a sticky bun to pile on the pounds. Her gold, naturally streaked hair stayed in the style into which she'd combed it, unlike Kathryn's wayward curls which did whatever they wanted to, no matter how much styling foam or hair lacquer she applied. Her complexion was the nearest thing to perfection that Kathryn had ever seen, whereas her own was sprinkled with freckles. Rosie had only one fault, and that was her blunt, often brutal candour, which Kathryn had been on the receiving end of more than once. In fact, Kathryn wondered now if that was what was frightening men away. She had grown accustomed to it over the years but it could still, every so often, intimidate her. So it was with an expression of defiance that Kathryn now returned her stare, silently preparing herself for the inevitably harsh criticism. 'I'm living at Willow Court.'

For the first time ever — well, as far as Kathryn could recall, that was — Rosie was completely lost for words. Her eyes widened until they were saucers — huge saucers at that; and saucers, moreover, that were fringed with enviably long and maddeningly curling lashes — something else that Kathryn would have been prepared to sell her soul to possess.

'Say something — anything,' Kathryn urged her.

But the angry explosion that Kathryn had been fearing didn't materialise. Instead, Rosie spoke with an uncharacteristic calm. 'Okay. Well, please correct me if I'm wrong, but doesn't Sebastian Grant still live there?'

'He does.'

'So — ' Rosie narrowed her eyes. ' — would you care to fill me in? You know, things like how you come to be living there, too?'

'I called in to see him on my way

home on Friday.'

'You called in?' Rosie burst out. Ah-ha, this was more like it, Kathryn decided. She stoically braced herself for further angry outbursts. 'To Willow Court? Why on earth would you do that?'

'I wanted to apologise.'

'What — after two and a bit years?'

'Yes, I've always felt guilty that we didn't make more of an attempt to stop what happened.'

'There wasn't time.'

'There might have been if we'd acted faster.'

'Kathryn, we couldn't possibly have reached her in time. We were yards away.' Rosie eyed her friend, her eyes again narrow with speculation. 'So did you apologise?'

'Yes.'

'And what did he say?'

'He was very nice.'

'Nice? Nice?' She hooted scornfully. 'Not an adjective I would have applied to Sebastian Grant. He devastated me;

literally flailed me. And I was already feeling bad enough, what with suffering regular flashbacks, not sleeping, and if I did manage it having the most horrendous nightmares. So how come you got away with it?'

Kathryn shrugged. 'Maybe because more time has elapsed, I don't know. Anyway, he said I — we had no need to apologise. In fact, he asked me to say how sorry he was about the way he spoke to you.'

'Huh, did he? It took him long enough. So what, he asked you to live with him as a sign of his remorse?'

'No. I offered to look after Jamie, his son. His nanny has left.'

'You offered to what? Are you completely mad?' Rosie burst out a second time.

'No — as I've just said, he seemed nice.'

'Yeah, yeah, yeah, you said that before. Tell me, has he also sprouted wings and a halo?' she scoffed.

'Of course not — '

'Oh, you do surprise me.' Rosie snorted derisively. 'So presumably he accepted your very generous — not to say, insane — offer? Seeing as you've already moved in?'

'Yes.'

'Why? Why would he accept such an offer from someone he'd never met before?'

'Because he's desperate and hasn't been able to find anyone else. It's only to be a temporary thing, anyway. He's still trying to find a qualified nanny.'

'Good grief, Kathryn, you don't even know the man. He could be a serial killer.'

Well, that was something her mother hadn't thought of, that Sebastian might be a serial killer. It was almost uncanny. Helen and Rosie could be mother and daughter, their reactions had been so similar; practically identical, in fact.

'Don't be stupid.'

'Okay, so perhaps that's a bit over the top, but he accepted your offer. Which makes me think he must have some sort of ulterior motive,' Rosie darkly muttered.

'Like what?'

'I dunno. Like seducing you? He does have a bit of a reputation where women are concerned. And not just since his wife died.'

The image of Linda kissing him surged into Kathryn's mind. Who knew what had gone on there? But she'd left to get married. She'd hardly have been having an affair with her boss. Still, Kathryn decided she'd better be on her guard at all times, just in case. At the first sign of anything untoward, she'd be out of that house so fast, a greyhound wouldn't catch her.

'I'm sure he wouldn't become involved with his son's nanny.'

Rosie snorted again. 'He's up to something, though. I'd put money on that. Did he seem overly interested in you?'

'No.' That wasn't strictly true. She had felt as if he were keenly appraising her in those initial few moments, missing nothing; not a single inch of her curvy figure. However, his attitude to her over dinner had gone some way to laying that sort of concern to rest. For a few moments then, he'd regarded her as if she were something nasty on the bottom of his shoe.

'You do know what he does for a living?' Rosie then demanded.

'Y-yes. He buys failing businesses.'

'Yeah, and then proceeds to sack the staff and strip the place of anything he can sell for a profit. The man has absolutely no principles.'

'That's not quite true. He explained what he does and it's not that simple. Anyway, as I've said, I'll only be there for a while.'

'Yeah, I know you did. My question now is, how long's a while?'

Kathryn shrugged.

'This is the guilt thing, isn't it? Kathryn, it's been over two years. Get over it. I have. There were other bystanders nearer to her than us; they could have done something but they didn't. I truly believe, in retrospect, that no one could have stopped her. And maybe Sebastian was to blame. Have you considered that? She must have been very unhappy to do such a thing.'

Matt had said much the same at the time, about it being Sebastian who should probably shoulder the blame. Could he and Rosie have inadvertently latched onto the truth — that maybe Sebastian Grant was the one at fault? That he had indeed made his wife so unhappy that she no longer wanted to live, not even for her son?

Kathryn looked away from her friend's furious face, only to find herself staring directly at the man in question. Sebastian Grant was standing, fortunately some yards away, at the bar, and looking straight at Kathryn and Rosie. Had he recognised Rosie? Heard what they were saying? Oh good Lord! How long had he been there?

She glanced at his companion, who was a very beautiful woman, impeccably made up and elegantly dressed

— over-dressed actually, for the Red Lion; it was only a fairly commonplace country pub. They must be having a drink before going on somewhere else. Obviously this was who he'd had to see: woman, and a beautiful woman at that. And he'd given the impression that it was some sort of business meeting. Although, she thought as she wrinkled her brow, to be fair, he hadn't actually said that.

Meanwhile Rosie, gloriously oblivious to the proximity of the man she was so forcefully castigating, ranted on. 'I bet he had affairs; bound to have. Dozens of them, in all probability. All that money, sinfully handsome . . . ' She snorted yet again, making no attempt to hide her contempt. 'No wonder his poor wife was driven to suicide,' she loudly declared.

'Rosie,' Kathryn hissed. 'For God's sake, he's over there at the bar. I hope he didn't hear you.' She slanted a sideways glance at him. Oh no, he was on his way over. He had heard. Oh

God, what would he do, or say?

Memories of how they'd parted just an hour or so ago — somewhat acrimoniously, it had to be said — re-visited her. If he'd overheard just a fraction of Rosie's diatribe, then her job, despite what he'd said, was toast — which, as it was only temporary, didn't really matter; and, as she'd decided no more than an hour ago, it could prove something of a relief. But then again if he was angry enough, especially in light of what she'd said earlier to him, it could mean that her father's and sister's jobs could also be in jeopardy.

She gnawed at her bottom lip, waiting for the killer blow to descend. However, contrary to her every expectation, all he did was smile and say, 'Kathryn, I didn't expect to see you here. You should have said you were going out.'

Was that criticism? Did she need to clear it with him before she went out for the evening? That wasn't the impression he'd given her. He'd said her evenings were her own. In the wake of her irritation, her words were cool. 'I didn't realise I had to notify you.'

'Oh, you don't. That wasn't what I meant. Presumably you told Joyce?' A frown creased his brow.

'Yes. Jamie's being looked after.' Her irritation dissolved. She couldn't blame him for worrying about his son. In fact, she could only give him credit for it.

'That's okay then.' His glance now slid to Rosie, a Rosie who had grown pale at the notion that he might have overheard her.

He held out a hand to her. 'Ms Mitton, I'm so glad to see you again. I feel I owe you an apology. I was extremely ungracious in light of your very kind visit. I hope you can forgive me.'

'Sebastian, darling,' a sharp voice interrupted. It was his glamorous companion, obviously vexed at being ignored. 'Shouldn't we be going? We don't want to be late.'

'Sorry, yes, you're right. I do apologise.' He turned back to Kathryn and Rosie. 'This is Cassandra, a friend. We popped in for a quick drink. Cassandra, this is Kathryn, who's helping me out with Jamie, and Rosie, her friend.'

Cassandra! was all Kathryn could think. *What sort of name is that? Why can't she simply be called Jane, or something equally commonplace? I mean — Cassandra, for heaven's sake.*

As if Cassandra had read Kathryn's thoughts, she barely spared the two women a glance, although her eyes did narrow slightly as they rested briefly on Kathryn. 'So-o, you're the new nanny.' She then averted her gaze once more, as if a mere nanny was someone too lowly for her to notice. The name of Rosie obviously held no significance for her.

'Um, no, not really,' Kathryn tried to protest.

Cassandra's gaze instantly returned to her. 'Oh, what would you describe yourself as then?' It was a blunt question, rudely asked. This woman clearly took no prisoners.

Sebastian intervened. 'Cassie, Kathryn is standing in as a favour to me and purely on a temporary basis, until I can replace Linda.'

'It won't be for long, I can assure you,' Kathryn curtly put in. 'I do have another job to go to, and it won't wait forever,' she blithely and quite erroneously said.

She felt rather than saw Rosie stare at her. 'You didn't tell me you had another — '

'I was about to,' Kathryn swiftly forestalled her. Of course she didn't have another job to go to, but no one apart from Rosie needed to know that.

Sebastian, too, slanted a look her way, because she'd told him she was currently unemployed, and had made no mention of another job waiting. However, he said nothing, to her relief. There was something about the woman with him that raised her hackles. The manner in which she'd called Sebastian 'darling', maybe? Although why that should irritate Kathryn, she couldn't have said. It was nothing to her who he saw in his free time. But the beautiful woman's presence at his side did rather reinforce Rosie's theory that his infidelity could have contributed in some way to his wife's tragic demise. Had Cassandra been in his life at the time of Sara's death? Could she, in fact, be the cause of the tragedy? She had a rather hard look to her — a glossy, fashion-plate look. Kathryn couldn't imagine her caring about anyone else. What she wanted — desired — would be paramount. A mere wife would be no obstacle, she was sure. Or was she being unfair? She didn't know anything about her, after all. Other than that she possessed an unpleasant, haughty manner.

'Can I buy you both a drink?' Sebastian asked.

'No, thank you, we don't want to keep you,' Kathryn immediately said. It was perfectly true; she wanted nothing to detain the other couple. In fact, the sooner they left the better.

'Okay, if you're sure.' Although it

seemed as if he'd accepted her refusal at face value, there was an intriguing little gleam to his eye as he regarded her.

It didn't stop Kathryn adding, 'We are,' however.

She watched Sebastian and his companion walking towards the doorway, Cassandra slipping her arm through his in a very familiar manner indeed. 'Thank goodness they've gone. I couldn't have stood another second in that — that patronising woman's company.' She glowered darkly after the couple. 'The faster they left the better, frankly. And I didn't think you'd want to accept a drink off him.'

Rosie didn't bother replying to that. She clearly had much bigger fish to fry.

'Well, there you have it,' she smugly proclaimed. 'If you want proof that he was making his wife unhappy by having affairs, I would say you've just had it, beyond any doubt. That poor woman. No wonder she threw herself under a lorry. And that's the man you've agreed to work for.' And she snorted for what seemed to Kathryn like the umpteenth time, swivelling her glance towards the pair disappearing through the doorway.

'Will you stop snorting like that,' Kathryn crossly said. Sebastian was, after all, a single man now, so there was nothing to stop him having a girlfriend. Cassandra's presence at his side proved nothing about his fidelity or infidelity at the time that his wife was alive.

'Well, here he is — was — with a woman at his side, and despite what you think, a very beautiful woman, if you like sophisticated and cool that is. Which clearly Sebastian does. I'd say it speaks for itself, so you can bet he was at it before.'

Kathryn felt she should at least try to defend him. 'Rosie, he's single now; there's nothing to stop him. Anyway, I'm sure she's just a friend, as he said.'

'Yeah, right! Did she look like just a friend? Give me a break.' Rosie started to snort again, but stopped mid-stream when she spotted Kathryn's expression.

'Believe me, she's more than just a friend. I'd stake money on it. And judging by the expression on your face at the moment, you think the same.'

'I don't. I know nothing about either of them and I care even less.'

'No?' She had the distinct impression that Rosie didn't believe her. 'Well if you want to be pedantic, it's true, we haven't actually had it from the horse's mouth. But I think we can hazard an educated guess as to her status.'

She may as well confess everything. Get it all over with in one go. 'I'm doing some PA work for him too.'

'My, my, he's really got you under his thumb, hasn't he? Who knows what he'll expect you to do for him next.'

'Rosie!' She disregarded the fact that, for the most fleeting of moments, she'd wondered the same thing herself. That was something she wasn't about to share, not even with her best friend.

'And where does Matt figure in this cosy little set-up?'

'He doesn't,' was Kathryn's blunt

response to that. She then told Rosie all about her and Matt's meeting. 'It's over, Rosie.'

She waited for the pain of her loss to begin. It didn't.

* * *

It was Thursday before Kathryn decided to have a look round the grounds of Willow Court. She hadn't had the time before, being so busy settling into her job — both her jobs. She'd spent the morning fulfilling her role of PA and it was now lunchtime — well, just after. She'd eaten with Jamie and Joyce and Jamie had then remained with Joyce.

Before she returned for the final hour of office work, she decided she needed some fresh air. It was a lovely, sunny afternoon, the sky an unbroken blue. She couldn't resist going outside. She'd make the time up. She was sure Joyce wouldn't object to keeping Jamie with her a little longer. She clearly adored him.

She opened the back door — the tradesman's entrance originally, she presumed — and walked out onto a wide, ornately paved terrace; it was the same one that led off from the library. It was considerably more extensive than she'd thought. In fact, it ran the whole width of the house at the rear, providing the base for various items of garden furniture, along with huge stone pots of skilfully arranged miniature shrubs and flowers. She wondered who'd planted them. Sebastian must employ a gardener for all of this, so probably he had.

Landscaped parkland stretched out in front of her as far as the eye could see. Joyce had told her that parts of it had been designed originally by Capability Brown; it showed. Groupings of ornamental trees, as well as many specimens of indigenous British trees, freckled the expanse of immaculately mown grass; closer to the house were huge beds of flowers. These were a riot of colour and scent: delphiniums, roses, perfumed stock, day lilies, and red hot pokers, to name just a few. She could even see an ornamental lake in the distance, complete with swans by the look of the white smudges on its surface. It all took Kathryn's breath away.

She started off across the grass, heading for what looked like an avenue of perfectly clipped yews, only to be distracted by the sound of a horse whinnying and hooves clattering on a hard surface. She stopped and glanced around her. The noise seemed to be coming from behind a high hedgerow, set quite a way from the house. She set off towards it but then stopped, belatedly uncertain about what she was doing. Suppose Sebastian was there? She didn't know where he'd gone once he'd issued his instructions for the day. Did she want to see him? More importantly, would he want to see her? Wandering into what he might consider his private domain, he might well view it as snooping; an intrusion.

Oh, what the heck! What if he did? This was to be her home for the foreseeable future; she was perfectly entitled to explore, wasn't she?

6

Once Kathryn had made up her mind, she wasted no time in striding towards where she thought the noises were coming from. She rounded the end of the hedgerow and found herself looking into a paved yard. A red brick stable block stood to one side and in front of this was a beautiful black thoroughbred horse, saddled and ready to be ridden. He was being led around by a small ruddy-faced man. She couldn't resist walking across to him and saying, 'Hey, how are you?' Man and horse halted, so she stretched out one hand to touch the lovely creature on the nose.

She grinned as the animal nuzzled her hand, clearly looking for something to eat. 'Sorry, I haven't got anything for you. I'll make sure I bring you something next time.'

'Aye, sure — he's a devil for the apples,

so he is. He'll have them out of your hand in no time,' the man remarked with a broad grin and a strong Irish brogue.

The sound of footsteps coming up behind them had both of their heads turning. It was Sebastian, dressed for riding in jacket and tight-fitting jodhpurs. Kathryn's breathing quickened — and not just at the sight of his muscled thighs. Would he object to her intrusion? View it as snooping, as she'd initially wondered?

Her anxiety, however, proved groundless, because all he did was look at the man and say, 'Ah, Jed, good, he's ready.' He turned to Kathryn and went on, 'So you found the way to the stables then. Meet Jed.' He indicated the still beaming man. 'He helps me out with Rory's care.'

'Rory!' she exclaimed. 'Unusual name for a horse.'

'Yeah.' He grinned. 'His full name is Emperor. Rory's easier.' He turned to the man holding Rory. 'And Jed, this is Kathryn.'

'Aah, the new nanny?'

'Well, only temporarily,' she replied.

He smiled amicably and then glanced back at Sebastian. 'I'll be off now, sir. I'll see you again tomorrow morning, first thing.'

'Okay, Jed. Thanks.'

'Enjoy your ride, sir.' He turned to Kathryn once more. 'Do you ride, Miss — ?'

'Kirkwood. But please, call me Kathryn. And no, I don't ride, sadly. He's very beautiful.' She stroked Rory's nose again.

The little man strode away with remarkable speed, given his small stature.

'Jed was a jockey, as you've probably guessed. He had to retire due to injury, so he helps me on a fairly regular basis.' He paused and, with his head tilted to one side, studied her for several seconds. 'Would you like to ride, Kathryn?'

Kathryn gave a start of surprise. That was the last question she'd expected him to ask. She'd wondered if he might demand to know if she'd completed her work, seeing as she was out here, wandering around. Or even ask where Jamie was.

'We-ell, sometimes I think so, but I've never had the opportunity.'

'Well, you have now. I'll teach you.'

That really shocked Kathryn. So much so, that she didn't at first know how to answer him. 'Um — well, I-I . . . ' she stuttered into silence.

Sebastian didn't seem to notice her uncertainty; he was far too busy giving her jeans and sturdy shoes the once-over. 'You'll do,' he said. 'So, want to give it a go now? It'll tell you whether you really want to or not. Just a few minutes, to see if you've got the aptitude for it. We could have a gentle walk round the yard; nothing too ambitious.'

A jolt of excitement stabbed at Kathryn. 'Could I?'

He laughed, and for a split second it was as if he and Kathryn were genuine friends, rather than employer and employee.

She felt a pang of excitement in the instant before common sense reasserted itself. *Don't get carried away*, she told herself. *It means nothing. You're still just his son's nanny and his PA.*

'Of course. Hang on, I'll go and get you a helmet.' He was back again almost at once. 'Here you are.' She fitted it onto her head and then he said, 'Right then. Foot in the stirrup.' He placed a hand on each side of her waist as she tried to do as he instructed. 'And then, heave yourself up.'

Heave herself up? She only just stopped herself from laughing out loud. The horse literally towered over her. How was she supposed to heave herself up, for heaven's sake? It would be like trying to scale a vertical rock face.

'That's it,' he said, as she finally succeeded in setting one foot into the stirrup. 'Now your other leg needs to go over his back, and that foot into the other stirrup.' He lifted her, his hands on each of her hips, pushing her upwards.

'Oomph!' she gasped as she plumped

down hard onto the saddle.

'There, that wasn't so difficult, was it?' He grinned up at her. 'Now, how does that feel?'

Mute with fright, all she could do was mutter, 'Okay, I think.' She didn't dare move; the ground looked perilously far beneath her. What if she fell off onto that hard surface? She'd break her neck, in all probability.

'Okay,' Sebastian said, 'now take hold of the reins while I make a couple of adjustments.' He fiddled briefly with the leathers that held the stirrups. Then, 'Okay. You're ready.'

And, all of a sudden, Rory was moving. Her fear was instantly forgotten as a sensation of pure exhilaration gripped her. She was actually riding. Sebastian stayed right beside her, keeping his hand on Rory, all the time issuing gently murmured instructions to the animal, as well as to Kathryn.

'Good?' he asked at one point.

'Great!' she cried. 'I could take to this.' And she could, she realised. She was loving it, now that she was up on his back.

'Well, maybe I could give you a lesson or two — or maybe Jed would be the better teacher? He is the expert, after all.'

Rory walked on, very slowly; very smoothly. It was as if he knew he had a novice on his back. After a moment or two, Sebastian removed his hand and stood a little way back, just watching her. 'Keep your back straight. Don't tug too hard on the reins. You're doing great, Kathryn; really great.'

Kathryn felt confident in that second that she could indeed learn to ride — until, unexpectedly, everything went wrong. As Rory began to turn to walk back the way they'd come, Kathryn's one foot slipped out of the stirrup and she felt herself begin to slide sideways.

'Oh no,' she cried, 'I'm going to fall . . . '

She didn't have to say any more. Sebastian literally leapt forwards, managing to catch her before she fell to the ground, which was how she found herself cradled in his arms, his breath feathering her face and the scent of his aftershave filling her nostrils. Blue eyes laughed down into hers as a set of gleaming white teeth flashed from between parted lips.

Kathryn's heart leapt into her throat, making it impossible to breathe; her pulses leapt into tumultuous life. She had her mouth open ready to thank him, when something very strange happened. Sebastian's smile fled as his face paled and his breathing, in stark contrast to hers, quickened. They stared mutely at each other, their faces a mere inch apart.

'Oh, go-goodness, sorry,' she eventually managed to stutter. 'I-I must be heavy.' It was the only thing she could think to say, mainly because he looked completely winded. Yet she wasn't that heavy, surely? Not for a man as powerfully built as he was.

Without saying a word he released her legs, and she found herself standing on the ground — shakily, it was true, but nonetheless she was upright. Mind you, that was probably due to the fact that his one arm was still around her. They stood, chest to chest, thigh to thigh, staring at each other, Kathryn acutely aware of the erratic pounding of her heart and the mad rush of blood through her veins. He must be able to feel her response, surely — he was standing so close. Her heart felt as if it was ready to burst from her breast.

'S-sorry,' she again said, somewhat foolishly.

'That's okay. Don't apologise.' He spoke stiffly, all trace of laughing friendliness gone. His eyes were steely slits, and his jaw had hardened till it bore a marked resemblance to a block of granite. He looked like a man thoroughly annoyed.

'Maybe I'm not cut out for riding after all.' She gave a weak laugh.

'Everyone has a fall now and again.'

Hah! She couldn't, for the life of her, imagine him falling off.

'Well, as I'm down now, I'll — um, I'll get back to the office.' She moved out of the circle of his arms. Again, he released her at once and she turned away, hurriedly heading back the way she'd come. Her heart was still pounding as she felt his gaze following her, searing into her back.

'Kathryn,' he suddenly called.

'Yes?' She glanced over her shoulder at him.

'Any time you want to ride, just ask Jed to take you.'

'Oh, right — well, I'll see. I wouldn't want to be a bother to anyone.' Disappointment that he hadn't offered himself as instructor sliced painfully through her.

His gaze measured her: hooded, glittering, sardonic almost, as he murmured, so softly that she only just caught the words, 'Oh, you'd never be that.'

She turned away once more, musing. Now what on earth did he mean by that? And what on earth had just happened between them? Had he simply been winded from taking her full weight as she fell? Or had it been something more? Something much more significant? Could he be attracted to her, as she was beginning to be to him? Surely that was impossible. He was outrageously handsome, and rich — he could have any woman he wanted. So why would he want her? Especially when he had the glamorous Cassandra, ready and waiting? She dismissed the possibility from her mind. It was nothing more than wishful thinking on her part.

* * *

It was Saturday before Matt finally phoned Kathryn. She'd begun to think he wasn't going to contact her again — not that she'd thought much about him at all. What had happened between her and Sebastian, in those last few moments together at the stable, kept returning to her, each time distracting her from whatever she was doing, and leaving in its wake a simmering sense of anticipation — an emotion she had tried very hard to quash with little success, sadly.

'We should meet,' were Matt's opening words, 'and talk.'

'Yes, we should,' she agreed. She had a strong premonition of what it was that Matt wanted to talk about. As she'd already told Rosie, it was over between them. As much on her part as his. Still, she owed it to him to meet him and conclude things properly. They'd once been as close as two people could be, after all.

They, too, met at the Red Lion. One look at Matt's face told her that her suspicions were correct. He looked guilty, evasive even, and he was rubbing the back of his neck, something he always did when troubled. 'So how's life at Willow Court?' he finally asked.

'Good. Jamie's an adorable little boy. It's no hardship to take care of him. How's life going for you here in

England? Must be a bit dull after Dubai.'

'Yes — well, no, I'm going back — on a five-year contract. Kathryn . . . ' He regarded her nervously, once more massaging his neck. He was clearly expecting some sort of bad reaction from her. When it didn't come, he went on. 'I've met someone else. Someone in Dubai.'

'I did wonder. You haven't been exactly eager to see me.'

'I'm sorry. I should have told you when it first started.'

'Yes, you should have. I wouldn't have wasted my time then, waiting for you.' He'd strung her along, kept her hanging on for his return, when all the time he'd had someone else. The nerve of him! 'Just for the record, how long has it been going on?'

'Twelve months.'

That made it round about the time that his phone calls had begun to drop off. She wondered then if he had asked for his contract to be extended. It would seem likely, given the circumstances.

'She's pregnant,' he went on, 'so we're going to get married.'

That surprised as well as hurt her. Matt had always been adamant he didn't want children, even when she'd told him she did. It had been the one aspect of their relationship that had troubled her. 'Th-that must have been a shock.'

'At first yes, but the more I think about it, the better it feels.'

'That must come as a relief, considering how you feel about having children.' Her tone was one of biting sarcasm; it seemed the only way to disguise the ache of pain that she was feeling, despite having already guessed that he'd moved on and their relationship was over.

A spasm of misery momentarily crossed his face, making her wonder if he was quite as happy about it all as he made out.

She glanced towards the bar, quite

unable to look at Matt any longer. If they'd married, would he have gone on denying her the family she wanted? Maybe not, because here he was, eagerly anticipating the pleasures of fatherhood. Still, she couldn't help but feel pain that another woman had been able to change his mind so effortlessly. That didn't last long, however, because she saw Sebastian standing there, just as he had been the other evening.

They'd continued to eat dinner together each night, Kathryn making sure their conversation was restricted to the commonplace, mainly what she and Jamie had been doing together. They sometimes progressed to discuss their favourite books, music — food even on one occasion, mainly at Sebastian's instigation. It turned out he loved any sort of seafood — 'I sometimes think I'll turn into a lobster,' he'd laughed one evening. 'What about you?' he'd gone on to ask. 'What's your favourite?'

She'd said, 'Not fish, not usually. I like pasta, or a steak when I'm in the mood. I love roast lamb, but when I'm eating out I quite often opt for one of the vegetarian dishes.' He'd even tried to draw her out on her family a couple of times but Kathryn had remained reticent on that subject, considering it too sensitive a topic, seeing as he also employed both her father and sister. One thing he'd never mentioned was the incident at the stables, when he'd held her in his arms. But then she hadn't expected him to, not really. She was pleased, though, that he regularly made the effort to be home to read Jamie's bedtime story to him. She couldn't fault him as a father, whatever his other failings might be. However, he had quizzed her about the new job she'd mentioned in the Red Lion, saying, 'You didn't mention that you had a job waiting.'

'No, I didn't. It's not important. They know I can't start yet.'

She felt her face redden. She'd always hated lying, and bitterly regretted having done so then. It was entirely down to

Cassandra's attitude towards her and her role in Sebastian's household. Still, she shouldn't have let it get to her. It had been childish.

'There is no other job, is there?' he softly asked.

'No,' she curtly conceded. She met Sebastian's amused look with defiance.

He let out a shout of laughter. 'I apologise for Cassie's manner. She can be a little . . . ' he was clearly searching for the right adjective.

Kathryn couldn't resist it. 'Snobbish?'

'Well a bit, I suppose. But I was going to say blunt.'

Kathryn snorted. 'Or even rude?'

He ignored that, going on to say, 'She's been brought up in a very wealthy family, with everything handed to her on a plate.'

'Along with a silver spoon to eat it with, no doubt.' Kathryn spoke sarcastically now. 'Lucky Cassie.'

Again, Sebastian didn't reply to that gibe. Instead, he changed the subject.

Kathryn felt ashamed. What on earth was the matter with her? She wasn't usually this — well, not to put too fine a point on it — bitter; envious, even. And it wasn't of the other woman's lifestyle, either. But she wasn't going to investigate what else it might be too closely. She had a very strong suspicion she might already know the answer.

Now, once again, she noticed that Sebastian was watching her — and Matt. His brow was drawn down into a frown as he studied them both. Did he sense what was happening between her and Matt? She wouldn't be surprised. The more she came to know Sebastian, the more she realised exactly how astute, not to say perceptive, he was. There had been times when she'd felt he could see straight through her; could read her every thought and that disturbed her. She preferred to keep some things to herself.

She glanced at his companion, a man this time, who also was scrutinising her and Matt. Sebastian said something to him and, just as he had the other evening, he walked across to her. The only difference now was he wasn't smiling.

'Won't you introduce me, Kathryn?'

'Of course. This is Matt Bradley. He's just back from Dubai.' Completely out of the blue and somewhat surprisingly, if not belatedly, tears stung Kathryn's eyes. Despite realising that her affections for Matt had cooled, his imminent departure to marry another woman and have a child with her made her think that he couldn't have ever loved her, Kathryn; not really. Not if he could cast her aside so easily. And that really did hurt.

'Kathryn — ' Sebastian's low tones drew her gaze to him. ' — are you okay?'

She nodded, afraid that if she spoke, her voice would shake and reveal her distress.

He laid a hand on her shoulder. She gave a soft gasp. The touch of his fingers made her heart miss a beat — well, several beats, in fact. She stared up helplessly into his face and her mouth parted as she acknowledged the unpalatable truth — a truth which she'd begun to suspect that first night at dinner and then afterwards in the pub. And finally, even more obviously, when she'd fallen from Rory and he'd caught her in his arms. She was growing more and more attracted to Sebastian Grant, which, as far as she could see, meant only more pain for her.

'Well, I'll leave you to your drinks. Nice to meet you, uh, Matt.' But his look belied the friendliness of the words. In fact, it almost seemed to contain a warning to Matt.

Not long after that, and right after Sebastian and his companion left, she and Matt parted for good. Matt would, in all likelihood, remain in Dubai after the five years. She'd probably never see him again. Belatedly, anguish swept through her at what had happened; at the finality of her and Matt's parting. One minute she'd been hoping for a proposal of marriage, the next that hope had been well and truly extinguished, and here he was, preparing to walk out of her life.

She drove back to Willow Court slowly, her thoughts preoccupied with the prospect of a life of spinsterhood and solitude, at least for the foreseeable future. She and Matt had spent so much time together up until his departure for Dubai. They'd enjoyed the same things, laughed at the same things, cared about the same things — and even though they'd been many miles apart, he'd always been there in the back of her mind. All that was at an end now, and she felt totally alone. Although why she should, she didn't really know. Her family were here, as were her friends.

Hot tears again stung her eyes, overflowing in this instance and running down her cheeks. Angry with herself for what she perceived as pathetic weakness, she dashed them away. Even so, her cheeks remained damp as she walked into Willow Court.

She wasn't particularly bothered by this, as she wasn't expecting anyone to be there to witness the evidence of her unhappiness.

But there she was proved wrong.

7

Sebastian was in the hallway — waiting for her? Maybe he was about to offer her more riding lessons? Either seemed highly improbable.

Again, she started to wipe her cheeks — in vain. Because Sebastian strode over to her, and using just his thumbs, did the job for her. His remaining fingers cradled her face, his expression as he did so a strange one; it was almost tender, yet at the same time full of anger. Could he be starting to care for her, as his sudden pallor and his quickened breathing at the stables when she fallen into his arms had seemed to suggest? No, it had to have been her imagination. The truth was he'd probably just been winded by being forced to bear the full brunt of her weight, as she'd initially thought. And after all, he had Cassandra; she'd seen that for herself.

'Has he hurt you?' His jaw tightened and his tone was a grim one.

She swallowed and shook her head.

'He has, hasn't he?'

'A bit, yes.' To her shame, the tears welled and spilled over yet again. Why was she so upset? She didn't love Matt any longer. 'H-he told me he's going back to Dubai.' She attempted a laugh and failed miserably; it erupted instead as a hiccup. 'To get married. He met someone else out there — and she's pregnant. Why didn't he tell me before? We'd been together for a year and a half before he went, and-and I've been waiting for him for the past two years,' she wailed. 'He-he never wanted children, that's what he said.'

'And you do.' His voice was low and soft; gentle. It was how he spoke to Jamie when Jamie was upset.

She gave a little sob and nodded.

'Oh, Kathryn, he's not good enough for you.' He was staring down at her now, his hands still cupping her chin, her cheeks. Her tears spilled down over them. He didn't seem to notice. 'Believe me, there's someone far better for you — ' His eyes had darkened until they were the colour of crushed blueberries, their expression compelling; magnetic, even. She couldn't seem to look away. Not even when his fingers began to stroke the skin of her face, caressing her.

She sighed, feeling . . . well, almost cherished. It felt so wonderful, so right. 'I hope so; I really do.' Her eyes widened helplessly as she looked up at him, her senses suddenly heightened to an almost unbearable degree. So much so, that a tiny pulse began to beat in her throat, catching her breath and halting it. She saw his gaze go to it.

'There is, I know it.' The words were a husky murmur as his head moved nearer to hers. His breath, just as it had at the stable, feathered her skin. She breathed deeply, drinking in the scent of him; a seductive man-scent. She closed her eyes beneath the onslaught of emotion that this induced, and, all of a sudden, he was kissing her: demandingly; passionately; pulling her close to him, so close she could feel every hard line of him.

This was what she'd wanted at the stables. There — she'd admitted it. Which was why she was powerless to stop what happened next. Her lips parted beneath his as she kissed him back and slid her arms up his chest to link her fingers at the back of his head, glorying in the feel of his hair against her skin, drowning in the rising tide of longing. He pulled her even closer, his hands moving over her, caressing, cupping, just as a small cry sounded from upstairs. It was Jamie, calling her, crying — while she was —

She pulled away. What was she doing, responding to his kiss so, so eagerly? Whatever must he think of her, to surrender so readily? She didn't look at him as she spoke. She couldn't. Her face burned with shame at her weakness; at what she belatedly viewed as her immodest — cheap? — behaviour.

'That-that's Jamie. I must go. Sorry, I don't know what — '

'Kathryn, look at me.'

She did; once again, she couldn't help herself, despite dreading whatever she might see upon his face. She wouldn't be able to bear it if it was contempt at her willingness to be kissed by someone who was little more than a stranger still. But his expression was unreadable.

'It was just a kiss. But I'm sorry too. I've embarrassed you and I shouldn't have.'

Her heart sank. Was that all it was? Just a kiss?

Well, it might have been just a kiss for him; for her it had been nothing short of a revelation. For it had made her realise that she was more than attracted to him; she was in serious danger of falling in love with him. And where did that leave her? Precisely nowhere. For there could never be anything between her and Sebastian. They were so far apart, they may as well be on different planets: he with his immense wealth, she with virtually nothing, not even a proper job. And she was his son's nanny and his PA, for goodness sake. It was practically a cliche.

She tore herself free, muttering, 'Of course — just a kiss, right,' as she made for the stairs and Jamie's bedroom. Thank goodness tomorrow was Sunday. She'd go home and see her family. Restore the precarious balance of her life at the present time to normal. Although, she asked herself, could things ever be normal again? She thought not. Sebastian was having far too big an impact on her for that. She should never have offered to come here. Whatever had she been thinking of? It was turning out to be the biggest mistake she'd ever made.

* * *

She left the house early the next morning, thankfully without as much as a glimpse of Sebastian. She didn't know how she'd face him after what had happened between them the previous evening. It had been bad enough to find herself tumbling into his arms at the stable. But then last night, to respond so eagerly, willingly, to his kisses; to allow him to caress her intimately, almost — what had she been thinking of? She hadn't been thinking, that was the trouble. She'd allowed her passions to override her senses and those kisses had been the shameful result. But what was really hurting was the casual way he'd — not to put too fine a point on it — dismissed what had happened between them. It might have been just a kiss to him; to her, it had been much, much more.

He hadn't followed her up to Jamie's room, although she'd felt his gaze on her as she'd left him, so she'd comforted the little boy and settled him down to sleep once more before she went to her own room.

Now she could hear Jamie talking to Joyce in the kitchen as she silently let herself out of the front door and all but ran to her car.

Her mother and father were sitting drinking coffee when she arrived. Unusually, they weren't talking. Her father was absent-mindedly chewing a biscuit; her mother, her elbows resting on the kitchen table, chin cupped in hand, was staring blankly ahead. As for Jess, as was her habit on a Sunday, she was obviously still in bed.

Kathryn felt a stab of misgiving. It was so unlike her mother to be silent like this. Normally she chattered away like a troubled magpie.

'Kathryn,' her mother remarked, 'you're early.' She'd rung them the evening before in the wake of her disturbing encounter with Sebastian to say she'd be back for the day. Her mother had been stand-offish with her so Kathryn could only presume that she hadn't yet been forgiven for going to help Sebastian.

'Yes, I thought I'd spend as much of the day with you as I can. What's the news about the thefts, Dad?'

'Oh, you mean your employer doesn't keep you informed,' her mother snapped. 'Oh, silly me. Of course he wouldn't — you're just the help, aren't you? So he's hardly likely to do that.'

Richard said nothing. He put his half-eaten biscuit onto his saucer and simply looked at his wife, his expression one of rebuke — which Helen chose to completely disregard. In fact, she barely looked at him at all. Richard, somewhat pointedly then, turned his attention upon Kathryn as if to demonstrate to his wife that she was his daughter and he would support her in whatever she chose to do. He looked strange, though; edgy even, as if he was reluctant to discuss the matter.

'There isn't any. Well, not really,' he finally told her.

Helen snorted. Richard ignored her.

'Some more food has gone missing,' he then went on. 'Not a huge amount, but still it's troubling. The truth is we don't even know how it's being done.

I'd have thought our spot checks would have deterred anyone from smuggling as they leave. But if it's being done overnight, with no signs of a break-in, then that means someone must have got hold of some keys, and that's infinitely more worrying.' He glanced away from her then, his gaze as blank as his wife's had been only moments before.

Again, Kathryn experienced that stir of misgiving. 'But if it's being stolen overnight, even if someone does have keys, wouldn't whoever it was have set the burglar alarm off — unless they know the code, of course?'

'We don't have an alarm at the moment, that's the problem. It's been disabled. It kept going off for no reason and disturbing the neighbours. Grant is going to have a new one installed, more modern.' He shrugged. 'He thinks it's time to call the police, but I've managed to persuade him not to, not yet. I'm sure we can sort it out ourselves. I mean once the police are involved, and if they take it seriously, it will be a whole different ball game. They'll question everyone, seed even more suspicion amongst the work force, and that's the last thing we need. It's tense enough in the department as it is.'

Kathryn turned to Helen then, deciding to change the subject. Richard had looked increasingly uncomfortable the more he said. 'How are you, Mum?' She'd leave any further discussion of work until she was alone with her father.

'Fine. Why wouldn't I be?' Helen's tone was a defensive one.

'No reason. I'm just asking. You don't seem yourself.'

Helen didn't answer that. Instead, she stood up and busied herself preparing what looked like several pounds of cabbage and potatoes for lunch — far too much for just four of them in Kathryn's opinion. It was a blatantly self-protective strategy; she wasn't going to tell them what was wrong and that was that. She did say, 'Jess is bringing a friend for lunch.'

'Where is she, by the way? Still in bed?'

'No, she didn't come home last night.'

'Didn't come home? Where was she?' When her mother ignored her question, she turned to her father.

He shrugged. 'Your mother spoke to her, not me.'

'Mum?'

'She stayed at some friend or other's house. She rang me this morning.'

'Did you know she was going to stay out?'

'I guessed when she didn't come back.'

Kathryn felt a tug of real anxiety then. It effectively banished her unease about her father and his situation at work, replacing it with a deepening concern about Helen. This careless attitude to her younger daughter's whereabouts was so unlike her controlling mother. At her sister's age and beyond, Kathryn would have been in for a real telling-off if she'd stayed out without warning. In fact, she'd most likely have been grounded for a week or two — no, make that a year or two!

Once again, she decided that something was definitely going on here. Could her mother really be having an affair? Because her mind certainly wasn't on her family. Yet, Kathryn simply couldn't imagine that happening, not in a million years. Helen had always been so contemptuous about anyone doing such a thing, so how on earth could she herself be doing it now? It simply didn't add up.

She glanced at her father, seeking some sort of support. Surely he was going to say something? But he was on his feet and heading for the back door. Still, the dejected slump of his shoulders told Kathryn that he was every bit as worried as she was. So, why didn't he demand to know what was wrong? An answer presented itself almost at once. He had enough on his plate at Supreme Foods without delving too deeply into possible trouble at home. And she couldn't really blame him.

Jess finally strolled in at one o'clock, accompanied by a long-haired, scruffily dressed youth who looked about the same age as her. He had purple-and-green streaked hair and studs, and piercings adorning every possible part of his body that was visible, as well as several tattoos all the way up each arm. Helen didn't evince any surprise so she must have met him before. Even so, Kathryn would have expected her mother to express some sort of disapproval of her youngest daughter's choice of companion.

Another sign that all was not well?

'Kathryn, this is Fitz. He works with me at Supreme Foods — well, not side by side with me. He packs and loads the vans. I didn't think you'd be here,' she then said to Kathryn, with what sounded like contempt. 'Not been chucked out already, have you?' She smirked.

'No, it's my free day. Hello, Fitz.'

'Hi.' His jaw began to work furiously as he chewed something in his mouth.

'Jess, um, take Fitz into the sitting room,' Helen said. 'Kathryn and I will be through in a minute. Your father's in his shed.' Her tone was a scornful one. 'Where he always seems to be these days.'

'Yeah, well, if you didn't go on at him non-stop, he wouldn't be, would he? It's either that or you completely ignore him.'

'Jess,' Kathryn cried. 'That's enough.'

'And who are you to tell me what's enough?' Her eyes blazed at Kathryn. 'You haven't been here to hear it all. Lately, it's been worse than the war in Afghanistan — You never know when the bomb's going to detonate.'

'Jess, go and call your father — now,' Helen abruptly commanded.

'You call him,' Jess bluntly retaliated as she followed Fitz from the room.

Kathryn stared after her sister, horrified by the way she'd just spoken to both her mother and herself. What was wrong with everyone? The family that despite Helen's authoritarian tendencies had always been close-knit seemed to be disintegrating before her eyes. She'd long ago accepted that she and Jess would never be really close — the eight-year gap between them had seen to that — but even so, at the moment things seemed to have reached an all-time low.

'Mum?' She glanced back at Helen. Helen was standing staring through the window, her shoulders slumped, her arms crossed across her breast. 'Are you going to let her speak to you like that?'

'Yes. I can't be bothered anymore. I haven't the energy. And she's right, you haven't been here.' Helen's voice shook.

'Mum? What's going on? This isn't like you.'

'Oh, just leave me alone, Kathryn. The last thing I need is you nagging.' Her words petered out, almost despairingly. 'I'm going upstairs. Keep an eye on the lunch in the oven. The potatoes need putting round the meat in five minutes.' And with that, Helen almost ran from the room, low sobs erupting from her.

Kathryn stood stock still. It sounded as if her mother and Jess thought she'd deserted them. Why would they think such a thing? All right, she'd left home, but she'd kept in regular touch, texting Jess and phoning her parents on a weekly basis. She hadn't visited as often as she should have, she guiltily conceded, mainly because she couldn't bear to be here without Matt. But if anything was wrong, why — why hadn't someone said something? She'd have returned immediately; they must have known that.

She placed the potatoes around the meat and returned the pan to the oven with hands that were dangerously shaky. Then, with a heart that was hammering in her chest, she followed her mother upstairs.

She didn't knock, which under normal circumstances she would have. However, these weren't anything like normal circumstances, so she simply opened the door. And there was Helen, blouse and bra discarded onto the nearby bed, standing in front of the mirror, closely inspecting something at the front of her.

'Mum, what's wrong? And don't say nothing, because that is simply not true. The way you're behaving — you're all behaving. I mean, look at you now. What are you doing? I'm not leaving until I know, so you might as well tell me right now.'

Helen swivelled to face her daughter, pointing to her uncovered breast. 'There — you see, a lump. I don't know what to do. Oh Kathryn, I'm so afraid.' She collapsed weeping onto the bed. 'It's all I can think about.'

Kathryn flew to her and, ignoring her own growing sense of dread and fear, sat alongside her, pulling her mother into her arms. Helen clung to her. Kathryn's alarm intensified. This helplessness was so unlike Helen. She'd always despised what she described as 'snivelling weakness'.

'Oh, Mum, Mum, why haven't you said something, at least to Dad? Ha-have you seen the doctor?' Her voice quivered as she faced up to the implications of what her mother had just told her. This couldn't be happening, not to them. Her mother might a bit of a control freak, but she loved her. She wouldn't be able to bear it if-if, well, she lost her.

'No.' Helen sobbed unrestrainedly as she slipped her bra back on, then her blouse. Her fingers shook as she buttoned it up once more. 'I'm too scared. What-what if it's cancer?'

'And what if it's a benign cyst?' Kathryn gently pointed out, all the while silently praying, *Please God, let it be that*. 'You have to find out. You can't go on like this.' It explained Helen's uncharacteristic behaviour, however. 'Why haven't you told Dad? He's so worried about you.'

'What was the point in both of us being afraid?'

'He's your husband; he loves you. We all love you. He'd-he'd want to know.'

'So why hasn't he pressed me to tell him? What's the matter with him?' Helen sounded angry now rather than afraid. 'Doesn't he care?'

'Of course he cares. As I've just said, he's terribly worried about you.' This also explained why Helen wouldn't allow him to touch her. He'd have felt the lump and insisted she saw the doctor. 'I presume Jess doesn't know either?'

'No, and I don't want her to — not yet. Not until she has to.'

'Okay,' Kathryn agreed, somewhat reluctantly. It could be that Helen's recently unusual behaviour was having its effect upon her younger sister too. Still, if that was what her mother wanted, it was her decision. 'I won't say anything.'

'Thank you. And I'm sorry I've been so hard on you. I tend to forget you're a grown woman. You need your independence; your own life. I'll try and remember that in future.' And she gave a watery smile.

'Oh, Mum. It's okay. I know you care about me and just want the best for me.'

Helen tenderly touched her daughter's cheek, giving Kathryn real hope that things might change for the better from now on; that Helen would, at least, try and moderate her dictatorial behaviour. She'd made a promising start with her apology and tender gesture.

'I want you to ring the surgery tomorrow,' Kathryn went on, 'and make an appointment. If you don't, I will.'

'You're right. Deep down, I've always known I'd have to in the end. I've been so silly.' She peered anxiously at Kathryn. 'But I worry about you working for that man. Is it dreadful? He has such a bad reputation, you know. It's said that he's completely ruthless and doesn't care about anyone, only himself.'

'Mum, he isn't like that at all. And if you could see him with Jamie . . . Well, it's obvious he loves his son deeply.'

Helen was mopping her tears away now, but still managing to watch her daughter closely as she did so. 'You won't get too attached to them, will you? Or you'll find it very painful to leave — especially the little boy. Children have a way of wrapping themselves around your heart.'

'I know, which is why I'm going to keep my distance.' Huh! It was far too late for that. She already loved Jamie intensely, and was in imminent danger of feeling every bit as deeply about his father. But what could she do? Her conscience wouldn't permit her to leave until Sebastian found a replacement nanny, and that didn't seem very likely at the moment. In fact, she'd begun to wonder whether he was even looking for someone. Certainly no one — as far as she knew, that was — had been to the house for an interview.

'Come on,' she said to her mother, 'let's go downstairs and I'll go and get Dad.'

'Oh, dear, what a fright. I'll have to

wash my face first.' Helen was gazing into the mirror again, only this time she was staring at her reddened eyes and blotchy cheeks. She swung back to Kathryn, looking more like herself again. 'But never mind me. What do you think of that boy? He's always here with Jess; they wander in and out at any time of the day and night. I can't keep up with it. In fact, I'm beginning to wonder if he's got a home of his own.' She frowned. 'He's not right for Jess. Do you think I should say something to her? Stop her seeing him?'

'Bit difficult if they both work in the same place. He won't last, not if I know my sister and her mood swings. But Mum, I would keep an eye on who she's spending the night with. You know, maybe a phone call now and again just to check she's where she says she is.'

Helen sighed. 'I know, you're right. Oh, I'm so glad I've told you about the lump. It's lifted some of the weight off me. Your poor father — he's taken the brunt of my worry, I'm afraid. I'll tell him later. Although whether it'll make him feel better, I don't know.' She sighed heavily again.

Lunch passed off relatively smoothly. Kathryn even managed to hold a civilized, if brief, conversation with her sister. She desperately wanted to improve relations between them as well; make an effort to bridge the gap between them. For Helen's sake as much as anything else.

So with that in mind she said, even though they weren't to her taste — too ornate, too many dangly bits, 'Those are nice earrings, Jess.'

'Thanks. Birthday present from Fitz.'

Kathryn glanced at Fitz. He was staring down at his plate of food, pushing everything around and not eating any of it.

'Is something wrong with the food, Fitz?' Helen asked finally in exasperation.

'Yeah, I don't eat meat anymore,' he told her. 'And I hate cabbage.'

'Well, leave it then,' Helen impatiently said.

'Right, I will.' He pushed his plate away from him in visible relief.

Jess, too, immediately placed her knife and fork side by side on the plate. 'Yeah, I'm vegetarian too from now on. Come on, Fitz, let's go.'

'Just a minute, Jess.' This was from Richard, who'd been listening to the exchange with little more than mild irritation up until that second. 'Your mother has gone to the trouble of cooking this meal, and you will do her the courtesy of eating it.'

'No way.' Jess stood up. 'I'm not poisoning my body with animal flesh. We're off out.' And before anyone could say anything else, she and Fitz were gone.

Richard, too, got to his feet, intending to go after them, but Helen reached out a hand to halt him. 'Leave them, Richard. I don't want another row. Not right now.' She paused, glancing at Kathryn for support. Kathryn nodded encouragingly. 'Sit down. I've got something to tell you.'

8

It was after eleven by the time Kathryn returned to Willow Court. Helen had told Richard everything. Richard had been understandably shocked but had taken his wife into his arms, assuring her that together they'd get through whatever lay ahead of them. He, like his daughter, had insisted that she ring the doctor the very next morning.

Kathryn finally left them, hopeful that everything would be okay — providing, of course, that the lump in her mother's breast didn't turn out to be malignant. A stab of real fear knifed through her then. What would they do if . . . ? She dismissed all thoughts of what if. She must keep telling herself that her mother would be all right; the medical world could do such wonderful things today.

If only her sister's attitude would also

improve. It was true Jess had always been touchy, right from the time she could talk, but this insolence, especially to her mother, was something completely new. Could the problem be that with her mother's preoccupation with her own health worries and Richard's subsequent withdrawal from them both as a result, Jess had been feeling that no one cared about her? Or could it be that she was getting into bad company? Kathryn didn't want to pre-judge anyone simply on appearances, but looking at Fitz and the influence he appeared to be exerting over Jess — not for the good — it seemed to Kathryn that it looked highly probable. She'd have a talk with her sister herself, away from her parents if possible. Try to find out what was wrong. Maybe next Sunday?

* * *

But all of that was banished from her mind, at least temporarily, when the following morning the first thing Sebastian said was, 'I have to meet an associate today and I'll need you to take notes for us. Would you mind?'

He was business-like and detached, and she found herself wondering if this was how it was going to be between them from now on. Perhaps he'd decided he'd allowed things to become too intimate, or maybe her enthusiastic — no, let's call it what it was, she decided — unbridled and passionate response to his kiss had repelled him? Either way, he'd obviously resolved to restore their relationship to a purely professional one.

'Of course not. That is what you're paying me for, after all.' Her tone matched his in brusqueness. That would show him.

But if she'd expected some sort of reaction from him, she was disappointed. Because all he responded with was a perfectly calm, 'Well in that case, if you're ready, we'll go.'

'Oh — um, you mean right now?' She glanced down over herself and her brow creased into a frown. Was she dressed appropriately for a business meeting? True, her trousers were a pair of tailored grey ones, but her blouse was decidedly casual: pale pink cotton and short-sleeved.

'You'll do.'

Good grief. As she'd fancied more than once now, he really could read minds.

'We're meeting Jack Wainwright. He handles most of the admin for me when I decide to purchase a business.'

'Oh, I see. Is-is that what we're going to be doing?' She couldn't help herself — her tone was a critical one; censorious, even. Another ailing concern he could eventually make a fat profit from? That was good, she congratulated herself; keep the resentful hostility going. That way, she would smother any more dangerous emotions.

'Well, not today, no. It doesn't work that quickly. We're just going to meet and discuss the viability of actually running the business on a day-to-day basis; try to gauge the extent of its potential profit making ability.' He shrugged as if the whole matter were of little or no importance. 'We will go and have a look at the place, though.'

She almost said, 'And then decide how many employees you'll need to get rid of,' but didn't. She managed to still her tongue just in time.

However, as if to confirm her growing conviction that he could indeed read her mind, he said, 'This time there's no question of redundancies. The owner, Richard Wingate, wants to sell; he's retiring. My plans are to grow the business, in fact; take on more people. He's allowed things to run down somewhat. I intend to expand production, find new markets, move into the Far East maybe.' His expression now was a sardonic one. 'Happy?'

Kathryn shrugged. 'It's nothing to do with me. I probably won't be around to see it, in any case.'

'Well, who knows?' Sebastian murmured.

Kathryn looked at him, her glance sharpening. What did he mean by that? She decided to try and find out. 'You are trying to find a nanny for Jamie? I mean . . . '

For her own well being, she mustn't stay here too long. Extended proximity could prove a dangerous thing. She was already far too attracted to him for her own good, despite the resentment she felt over his dubious business practices.

'Of course,' he smoothly assured her. 'There's just no one either suitable or, more to the point, available at the moment.'

She eyed him with suspicion. That came out altogether too quickly; too pat. As if he'd been expecting the question and had the answer already prepared. He met her gaze with all the confidence and ease that he'd exhibited in response to her question apart, that was, from a quizzically raised eyebrow.

She decided not to press the matter. She had a strong suspicion that it wouldn't get her anywhere if she did. He was clearly well-versed in the art of procrastination. 'Okay, well, I'm ready if you are.' The very picture of efficiency, she hoped, she picked up her notepad and pen and slipped them into the handbag that fortunately she had with her, and followed Sebastian from the room.

Within minutes, they were driving along the dual carriageway that led to the motorway. They were travelling in a very luxurious Mercedes that looked capable of effortlessly outrunning most other vehicles, which in the hands of a careless driver could prove extremely hazardous. And let's face it, she had no idea of what sort of driver Sebastian was.

'Where are we going?' She hadn't thought to ask before now.

'A place called Norton Prior. We're meeting Jack at a hotel there.'

'I've never heard of it.' Kathryn frowned. She'd thought she was familiar with most places around here.

'It's near to Stafford,' he said. 'About three or four miles outside.'

She stared at him. 'Stafford? Bu-but that's miles away, a good two hours' drive up the motorway, isn't it?'

He slanted a glance at her. 'Is that a problem?'

'Well, not as such. But I won't be back at the usual time to take Jamie off Joyce's hands. I mean — ' She checked her watch. ' — it's already nearly eleven.'

'Joyce knows. She doesn't mind looking after him. She'll put him to bed.'

'Put him to bed?' she cried. 'How long are we going to be out for?'

'Five or six hours, maybe more if things take longer than I'd anticipated. But don't worry, I'll make sure you have lunch and probably dinner on the way back.' He didn't look the least bit concerned by her show of horror.

'Well, I'm hardly dressed appropriately for a meeting in a hotel, or for dinner later.' She gestured contemptuously at her outfit.

'It's a small country hotel, Kathryn,' he soothed. 'Stop worrying. Nobody will notice what you're wearing.'

Gee, thanks a bunch, she grimly reflected. Now he was implying that she wasn't worth looking at. Great! That would do wonders for her self-esteem. Was he deliberately trying to put her down? To squash any hopes that she might be entertaining regarding him and their kiss? He was obviously regretting it now. Well, he needn't worry, she decided mutinously; she had no intention of letting anything like that happen again — ever. She'd chop her arms off first.

Within moments, they'd joined the motorway and were instantly surrounded by an armada of thundering lorries as well as dozens of speeding motorcars. Kathryn closed her eyes in exasperation. If all this wasn't absolutely typical of a self-made, wealthy man. He clearly thought everyone — her included — was there simply to do his bidding. Mind you, he was paying her an extremely good salary, so she supposed he had a perfect right to expect her to comply with his demands.

Thank heavens her mother wasn't here, though. She could already hear her remarks. 'Well! Such arrogance. Who does he think he is? Didn't I warn you?'

But then the night she'd spent worrying about her family caught up with her, and her eyes stayed closed as she slept the sleep of the exhausted.

'Kathryn, Kathryn.' A hand was gently shaking her by the shoulder. 'Wake up.'

'Oh no.' She sprang awake to find herself staring dazedly into Sebastian's amused eyes.

'You can stop snoring now. We've arrived.'

'I don't snore,' she indignantly told him.

'Only very softly. Quite endearing, really.'

He grinned at her, the sort of grin that instantly catapulted her senses into a frenzy. What was he up to? One minute he was business-like and detached, seemingly determined to maintain a proper distance between them; the next he exhibited all the characteristics of an engaging Lothario. Why? Was it all designed to keep her off balance? Vulnerable? Because if it was, it was working. She didn't know what to expect from one minute — no, make that one second — to the next.

'We're at the hotel and Jack's already here. There's his car.' He pointed to a snazzy-looking Porsche parked on the other side of the small car park.

Kathryn silently snorted. There was obviously loads of money to be made for both of them by all this buying and selling if they could afford such expensive motor cars.

Gathering her wits about her, she climbed from the vehicle, her fingers swiftly tidying several wayward strands of hair, before tucking in her shirt which had worked loose from the waistband of the trousers while she slept, and all the while staring in horror at the Georgian building standing before her. It might be small and in the country, but it looked very expensive and very, very elegant. Again, she glanced down over herself. Why, oh why hadn't she insisted on changing into something smarter? She had no trouble visualising the type of woman who would frequent this place. Women like Cassandra: designer-dressed, immaculately groomed, sophisticated, and — well, just plain beautiful. She groaned silently. It was too late to do anything about it now. She'd simply have to make the best of things.

However, when she walked inside and was greeted with the sight of a couple of women dressed just as casually as she was, she relaxed and followed Sebastian through the elegant black-and-white tiled hallway into a stylishly furnished sitting room. A man got to his feet and waved. Jack, Kathryn assumed.

As they neared him, he held out a hand to Sebastian. 'Sebastian, old man, good to see you.' His glance then immediately slid to Kathryn. 'And you must be Kathryn. How are you? I'm Jack.' He removed his hand from Sebastian's grasp and proffered it to Kathryn.

Kathryn took it, murmuring, 'I'm

fine, thank you. Nice to meet you.'

'Good; good. Come on then, let's sit down. I've ordered some coffee and sandwiches — and here it comes.' He indicated the approaching waitress before turning back to Sebastian. 'I thought we could talk about things first here and then go and take a look at the factory. I've let Wingate know, so he's expecting us.'

They all took their seats in the comfortable winged armchairs which encircled a low table. The waitress placed the tray holding a coffee pot, sugar, cream, and three cups and saucers down upon it. There was also a large oval salver crammed with delicious-looking sandwiches.

'Kathryn,' Sebastian said, every inch the professional again, 'perhaps you would pour, and then we can get down to business?'

Sometime later, their discussion completed for the moment, Jack relaxed back into his chair and said, 'Well, now that's done, we can go and have a look at the place. I think you'll be keen, Sebastian.

As we thought, there's huge potential for development.'

'Let's hope so,' Sebastian remarked drily. 'So far I've only taken your word for that. I would hate to think I've wasted my time.'

As he spoke, he got to his feet. Kathryn followed suit, clutching her notepad in her hand. She had literally pages and pages of notes, all written in a mixture of long- and shorthand.

'You lead, Jack, and we'll follow,' Sebastian commanded as they walked out of the hotel.

It was another two hours after that before they left the factory. Kathryn was starting to feel tired. Her brain was a maelstrom of facts and figures, her fingers aching and stiff with the sheer amount of writing she'd had to do. She prayed she'd got everything down correctly. There hadn't been much demand for shorthand in her previous job, so her skills — or rather, what skills she had, as she'd never been particularly adept at shorthand — had become rather rusty. She sneaked a glance at her wristwatch. It was four thirty. She'd kill for a cup of tea — her mouth could have competed on equal terms with the Sahara desert for dryness — but from the look of things, there was very little chance of that.

Jack turned to her. She'd noticed the way in which his glance had repeatedly strayed to her during their time together. It was becoming increasingly obvious that he liked what he saw. Mind you, she also quite liked him. He wasn't as obviously good-looking as Sebastian, but there was a distinctly engaging air to him. His grey-blue eyes twinkled, and a lock of his dark blond hair kept dropping onto his forehead.

'So,' he drawled with a warm smile, 'how have you got on? Mind you, you look very efficient — as well as very beautiful.' He moved closer — much closer. Their shoulders touched.

Kathryn sensed, rather than saw, the manner in which Sebastian reacted to this. He stiffened and frowned.

Jack, however, seemed oblivious to his employer's — she presumed Sebastian was his employer? — displeasure and went on. 'I was wondering, would you like to come and have a drink with me one evening?'

It would be good to have a diversion from her increasingly disturbing thoughts about Sebastian, Kathryn decided, so she smiled back. 'I'd really like that.'

But it wasn't to be.

'Kathryn is fully occupied taking care of Jamie,' Sebastian curtly put in.

Kathryn turned to look at him, her eyebrows raised in surprise. Her evenings were her own; he'd made that very clear right from the start. However, when he met her look of astonishment with no sign of remorse for his high-handed dismissal of Jack's invitation, Kathryn said nothing to counter his statement. Maybe he didn't approve of his employees going out together? However, if Jack wasn't an employee, but a partner — which taking into account his relaxed manner towards Sebastian was a very real possibility — was it reasonable to obstruct their meeting socially?

She had her mouth open to fight her corner when Jack said, 'She must have a day off, surely? How about Sunday?' He was looking at Kathryn as he said this, his expression suddenly an intense one. 'I could ring you.'

Again, Kathryn was forestalled from answering by Sebastian saying, 'Kathryn, would you return to the car?' He thrust the key at her. 'I want a word with Jack before we leave.'

Somehow Kathryn managed to hide her irritation at his manner towards her. It wasn't that she wanted to see Jack particularly; it was the way that Sebastian had interfered. And, not least, the manner in which he'd done so, by high-handedly dismissing her. He'd managed to make her feel like the lowliest of employees — which was a damned cheek, considering that she was doing him a favour. Nonetheless, she accepted the key; but in so doing, defiantly and with exaggerated warmth, she smiled at Jack. 'It's been a real pleasure to meet you.' She held out her hand, which Jack eagerly took before leaning forward to drop a kiss upon her cheek. She didn't immediately pull away, despite sensing Sebastian's glare.

'I'll ring you at Sebastian's number,' Jack went on. 'Or, if you have a mobile phone — ?' Clearly he wasn't going to be discouraged from trying to see her again.

'I do.' And she quickly rattled off her number before Sebastian could interfere yet again. She really couldn't see why she shouldn't meet Jack if she wanted to. What business was it of Sebastian's? She wouldn't be working for him forever, after all. And, as she'd already decided, seeing another man — especially one as attractive as Jack — would take her mind off her dangerously deepening feelings for Sebastian, as well as Matt's hurtful betrayal.

She began to walk away, heading for the car which was quite a way from the factory — at the far end of the large car park, in fact, and tucked into a corner. However, she couldn't resist a backward glance at the two men. They were clearly having a heated discussion about something. It couldn't be about her, surely? If it was, Sebastian must be warning Jack off. Her heart leapt. He couldn't be jealous of Jack, could he? Jealous of Jack's attentions towards her?

With nerves that felt stretched to breaking point, Kathryn climbed into the Mercedes. Maybe she shouldn't have responded quite so warmly, enthusiastically even, to Jack. But then again, why not? She was single, unattached. Her heartbeat increased and her pulse rate did the same. Sebastian had been noticeably angered by Jack's attention to her, and every bit as angered by her responses. So, how would he behave towards her when he returned to the car?

She didn't have to wait long to find out.

He yanked the car door open and climbed in, slamming it once again behind him. Jack's Porsche raced by; he raised a hand to them and grinned.

'I would appreciate it,' Sebastian bit out, 'if you didn't flirt with my partner — not while you're working for me.'

She gasped. 'I wasn't flirting.'

He swivelled his head and stared at her, his eyes dark and narrowed. 'So what would you call it then?'

'Um, just being friendly.'

'Friendly?' he snorted. 'You were all over him.'

'I was not.' Kathryn's anger was rising now, along with a sense of outrage.

'Oh no? What about that kiss? You didn't have to — '

'He kissed me,' she furiously broke in, 'and it was just on the cheek.' Good grief, he was behaving like some sort of Victorian despot. 'It's the customary way of saying goodbye to someone.'

'Yes, someone you know well — not a complete stranger.'

'He wasn't a complete stranger. I'd just spent the previous few hours in his company.' She was shaking now with genuine rage. Who the hell did he think he was, telling her what she should and shouldn't do?

'Kathryn.' He spoke quietly, but his next words were laced with exasperation and something that sounded like bitterness. 'Jack has quite a reputation with women.'

'Reputation?' she cried. 'What, you mean he's taken a few out?'

'Rather more than a few.'

'We're not living in the nineteenth century, you know. I'm a big girl and more than capable of looking after myself.'

'You think so?' He studied her from beneath lowered lids; there was a disturbing glint to his eye. 'Don't forget I've seen you crying over one man already.'

'That was completely different,' she explosively countered, 'and nothing to do with you.'

He disregarded that statement. 'Jack fancies himself as a playboy. He'll pick you up, show you a good time, and then drop you again.'

'Maybe that's what I want,' she defiantly argued.

'Is it? Is it really?' His voice was low; his eyes smouldered at her.

She shrugged. 'Why not? It could be fun while it lasted.'

'Oh well if it's fun that you want, you're in the right place.' His top lip curled at her as he reached out to grab her by the shoulders and yank her roughly into him as he ruthlessly captured her lips.

Kathryn didn't react; couldn't react. This had been the last thing she'd expected in the light of his anger with her. He pulled her closer, grinding his mouth almost brutally over hers, forcing her lips apart and thrusting his tongue in between.

Kathryn heard someone groan — and realised it was her, but she couldn't help herself. She began to kiss him back. He forced her backwards, sliding an arm beneath her, until she was practically lying on her seat, the back of her head pressed against the door. His mouth left hers and moved down her throat, searching for and finding the V of her blouse and the tops of her breasts. She gasped as his lips scorched her skin, setting her body aflame as desire swamped her.

But then as suddenly as he'd grabbed her, he released her again. She lay still for a second, shocked at the abrupt cessation of their lovemaking, before she sat up, hurriedly straightening her blouse, struggling to control her breathing. Her eyes were wide and translucent as she stared at him, at a face that was so pale it resembled skimmed milk. His lips were a tight line, his eyes no more than slits. Nonetheless, passion blazed at her. Or was it anger again? Whatever it was, outrage suffused her.

She searched for something to say, something like, who did he think she was? Some sort of cheap tramp that he could make love to whenever he felt so inclined, and then stop — all without saying a word? She didn't, however. Instead, she watched him in silence as he turned away and started the engine.

The car leapt forwards, the tyres squealing loudly on the tarmac, and within seconds they'd left the factory and its car park behind.

Not a word was spoken throughout the entire journey home, and Kathryn had never before felt so unhappy, so desolate, not even when Matt had ended things between them. In fact she felt used; bruised — she lifted fingers that noticeably trembled to her mouth. Her lips felt swollen and sore.

But the burning question that repeated itself over and over was, How could she possibly go on working for him after this? Such a thing seemed impossible to contemplate.

9

What on earth was she going to do? Kathryn asked herself as she went up to her room. Her stomach rumbled noisily and she realised they'd had no dinner. Well, she'd have to go hungry. She wasn't going down to the kitchen and risk bumping into Sebastian. Maybe she should just pack her bags and leave right now. But that would mean abandoning Jamie without as much as a goodbye, and she couldn't bring herself to do that. None of this was his fault. Which meant that, unless Sebastian himself ordered her to go, somehow she had to find the will as well as the strength to carry on. With the decision made, she managed to get some sleep, but it didn't stop her feeling deathly tired and extremely depressed the following morning.

However, she put it all to one side

and got Jamie out of bed, gave him his breakfast and responding cheerfully, as she always did, to his non-stop chatter. In fact, she was laughing at his antics as he helped her clear their dishes away when Sebastian strode into the kitchen.

Kathryn immediately stopped what she was doing and waited, barely breathing, for the words of dismissal. He was surely going to send her packing. His expression was one of determination, underpinned by something she couldn't identify. If she'd been pushed to say, she would have described it as discomfiture, and she knew that couldn't be so. There was no way that someone as self-confident as Sebastian would even recognise, let alone entertain, such an emotion. So it must be something else entirely.

Jamie, however, saw nothing of this, and cried, 'Daddy, Daddy, I'm helping clear up.'

'So I see. That's splendid.' But all the time he was talking, his gaze remained on Kathryn. She turned away, feeling unable to look at him while he dismissed her. Instead, she carried on putting things back in cupboards. Joyce was off doing something else. Kathryn longed for her to walk back in — anything to dispel the tension that was practically crackling round the room.

'Kathryn,' Sebastian said in a low voice.

She didn't look around, but carried on with her task.

'Jamie,' Sebastian said, 'would you like to go to your room? I need to speak to Kathryn.'

So he wasn't going to sack her in front of his son then. That was a relief.

'Okay,' she heard Jamie say.

Kathryn did turn her head then. 'I'll be up in a minute, darling.' Her voice shook. Would she be seeing him to say goodbye? The mere notion almost broke her heart, as she admitted that she'd allowed herself to grow far too attached to the small boy.

Once they were alone, Sebastian

moved towards her. Instinctively, she stiffened. This was it. She turned to face him. Never let it be said that she was a coward. She waited for the words that would mean she'd probably never see him or Jamie again.

'Kathryn,' he again said, 'I want to apologise to you.'

The shock was so great she couldn't speak. An apology was the last thing she'd anticipated.

'My actions yesterday were completely out of order. I'm sorry. I don't know what came over me.' He gave a mirthless grin. 'Well, that's not true. I do know, but . . . '

Kathryn stared at him, expecting some sort of enlightenment as to his reasons for what he'd done — other than rage, of course. However, when that failed to come, she waited in silence for him to go on.

'Anyway, I'm sorry. I hope it won't drive you away. Jamie needs you.'

Aah — Now we're getting to it, she bitterly reflected. He didn't want to drive her away, because then who'd look after Jamie for him? Joyce couldn't manage it full-time; she had the house to run. He wasn't really sorry at all. It was all just words; self-serving, insincere words.

'If you wish to see Jack then that's up to you.'

'Yes, it is,' she quietly said. 'I'm a single woman and free to — '

'Quite.' He bit out the word. 'I would appreciate it though if you didn't bring anyone back here.'

'Of course I won't,' she indignantly retorted.

'Thank you. I'll see you later then.' And with that terse little remark, he was gone.

* * *

It wasn't long afterward that Willow Court had a visitor — Sebastian's widowed mother, Olivia. Jamie was particularly thrilled. He clearly adored his grandmother and she just as clearly adored him back.

'Kathryn, isn't it?' She'd walked into the sitting room, where Kathryn and Jamie were sitting reading one of his favourite books. Kathryn nodded.

'So how are you finding working with my son and grandson?' she asked.

'Very enjoyable,' Kathryn truthfully replied. 'Jamie is a gorgeous little boy.' She deliberately didn't mention Sebastian. Not that there was really anything to say. She'd seen almost nothing of him since his apology in the kitchen. He was obviously avoiding her. Well, that suited her. She needed space from him, space and time to rid herself of her growing feelings for him.

'What's 'gorgeous', Kathryn?' Jamie asked.

Kathryn smiled at him. 'Lovable, irresistible — '

'What's irr-irristible?'

'You are.'

Olivia smiled at them both. 'Yes, he is gorgeous, isn't he? Just like his father was at that age.'

Kathryn tried to picture Sebastian at Jamie's age, but found it impossible. Images of how he looked now kept getting in the way.

'Sebastian tells me you've not been at Willow Court long. What did you do before coming here?'

It was very tactfully done, but Kathryn sensed the older woman's curiosity about her and wondered what else Sebastian had said about her. However, she didn't mind telling Olivia what she wanted to know, and once she'd finished, Olivia told Kathryn a little about herself.

'I live in Cornwall now, on the south coast, at a place called Fowey, and have done ever since my husband, John, died. We used to regularly holiday there and John and I loved it, so I have many happy memories to sustain me. You'll have to get Sebastian to bring you and Jamie down. I have a house overlooking a beautiful harbour. There are beaches nearby, and the Eden Centre to explore.'

'Well, I probably won't be here for much longer. I'll be leaving as soon as Sebastian has found a permanent nanny. I'm not a professional.'

Olivia looked surprised. 'Oh — well, that's a shame. It's quite obvious that you and Jamie are very fond of each other.' She looked thoughtfully at Kathryn and went on. 'Such frequent changes aren't good for children, especially one as young as Jamie is. Of course, what he really needs is a mother — someone permanent in his life.'

Kathryn held her breath, wondering what was coming next. But when Olivia said no more, Kathryn found herself wondering if it could be that she'd met Cassandra and was now considering her as a possible step-mother to her grandson.

* * *

The following day was Sunday so Kathryn decided to visit her parents. She was anxious to find out what was happening with regards to both her father's situation at work and her mother's problem. And then, of course, there was her sister.

Nothing, however, had changed. Not that there had been long enough for anything dramatic to take place. Her mother had managed to see her doctor, who had referred her on for tests. Her father was still the same, quiet and noticeably anxious. As for Jess, she wasn't even there.

'She's at a friend's house till later this evening,' Helen told her, 'and yes, I did check, so you can stop worrying.'

All in all, it was a fairly uneventful day. They lounged around in the garden; Helen cooked the usual ginormous lunch and then laid out an equally huge tea. Kathryn ate far more than she should have, and by the end of the feast she was convinced she'd gained several pounds in weight. She eventually returned to Willow Court, surprisingly glad to be back, considering the events of the past week or so.

As she walked across the hallway, intending to go straight to her bedroom, she heard the sounds of voices coming from the sitting room: they were those of Sebastian and his mother. She'd go in and bid them both good night but wouldn't linger. However, the impatience which she could detect in Olivia's tone stayed her footsteps.

'For heaven's sake, Sebastian, tell her how you feel. She won't know unless you do. Why do you feel impelled to keep your feelings so well hidden? It makes you appear cold; heartless, even.'

'Well, maybe it does, but I don't wish to broadcast my emotions. I will tell her, but in my own good time.'

'Oh, really.' Olivia was sounding even more exasperated by this time. 'What's the problem? Jamie needs a mother, darling — you know that yourself — and you need a wife. She'd be — '

Kathryn drew back. This wasn't the moment for intrusion. She shouldn't have lingered, eavesdropping on such an intimate conversation.

Slowly, she climbed the stairs. She could still hear Olivia, although her words were no more than a murmur. She was clearly pressing her son to declare his feelings for someone. But who did she mean? Who was it she was urging him to marry? Cassie? It seemed more than likely. Unless there was someone else in Sebastian's life? He'd never mentioned anyone else. Crushing misery engulfed her at the notion of him marrying Cassie. Kathryn simply couldn't imagine her as a loving, caring mother to Jamie. A swelling of pity for the small boy replaced the sensation of misery. Olivia was right about one thing, though: Jamie did desperately need a mother. Just not someone like Cassie. Yet, if Sebastian did indeed love her, which was beginning to sound very probable — ?

Again, sleep eluded Kathryn. And when she did finally drop off, dreams of Sebastian, Cassie and Jamie plagued her, always with Jamie sobbing and calling, in vain, for his mother.

Unsurprisingly, come the next morning, Kathryn was hollow-eyed with exhaustion. Sebastian greeted her with frowning suspicion and the growled words, 'What time did you get in last night?' He obviously thought she'd been out on the town with someone.

'About nine o'clock.'

His face darkened with an expression that had her wondering if he suspected that she'd overheard his mother and him talking.

'I went straight up to my room,' she told him. She didn't want him knowing that she had indeed been listening.

Although he struggled to hide it, it was definite relief that she glimpsed then. Although why he should be so concerned as to what she'd heard, she couldn't think. She was sure he'd consider their discussion none of her business. Maybe he was afraid that if he declared his intention to get married, she'd leave. And, she supposed, that wouldn't suit — especially with regards to his failure to find a professional nanny. Even he, as in love as he must be, could surely see that Cassie wouldn't welcome the responsibility of caring for a small, extremely lively and highly inquisitive boy.

'Could you help me out with a few things this morning? My mother will take care of Jamie.'

'Of course, I fully expected to.'

The morning literally flew by, and it wasn't until after three o'clock that Kathryn eventually stopped work. She went to the kitchen to ask Joyce where Jamie and his grandmother were.

'They've gone for a walk,' Joyce told her. 'It's such a lovely afternoon, they didn't want to waste it.'

'I thought maybe I could join them. Where did they go?'

'Haven't a clue. Why don't you sit and have a nice cup of tea instead? I'm sure they'll be back soon. I'll bring a tray to the sitting room.'

'Thank you, but I'll have it in my room, if that's okay. I need to make a phone call.' As she spoke, she heard the phone ringing in the library. Sebastian had gone out a couple of hours previously — on business, he'd told her.

'I'll just answer that,' she said.

'Hello.' She recognised the imperious tone instantly. It was Cassie. 'I want to speak to Sebastian.'

Kathryn felt a spurt of annoyance. A 'please' would have been nice. Still, it was on a par with the other woman's rudeness towards her on their one and only meeting at the pub. She evidently regarded Kathryn as little more than a servant and, as such, not deemed worthy of a show of good manners.

'He's not here,' Kathryn replied with equal bluntness.

'Well — ' Cassie's vexation at that transmitted itself down the line. ' — where is he? He was supposed to be meeting me at two. We were going to have lunch. It's now a quarter past three.'

'I really have no idea.'

'No, I don't suppose you have.' Her tone was one of contempt.

Kathryn felt her hackles rise.

'After all, he'd hardly tell the nanny his business.'

Kathryn was sorely tempted to put the receiver down at once, thus terminating the call. 'I do actually act as his PA.'

From the silence that greeted her remark, it was evident that Cassie hadn't known that. Kathryn couldn't help her gleeful smile, even though Cassie was unable to see it. So Sebastian didn't tell Cassie everything, then. Mind you, if he was intending to marry her — and she was as jealous and possessive as she sounded — he probably wouldn't want to risk upsetting her.

'I would have thought he'd have rung you, if he was going to be late. Have you tried to get him on his mobile?'

'Of course, that was the first thing I did. It's on answer service.'

'Then I can't help you, I'm afraid. I can take a message.'

'Don't bother. He's just arrived.'

And that was that. The line went

dead. Kathryn stared bemusedly at the receiver before she replaced it. What a thoroughly obnoxious woman. She couldn't believe that Sebastian could actually be planning to marry her; could, in fact, love her. But Olivia's words could only have meant that. Yet he'd kissed Kathryn — twice now. Well, obviously he'd only been toying with her. He'd made that very evident when he'd carelessly dismissed their first kiss and failed to mention the second, other than to apologise for his behaviour; and whether that had been for his anger over Jack's overtures to her or the fact that he'd kissed her so brutally, she had no idea. Anyway, one thing she did know: neither occasion had meant anything to him, other than something to be regretted and subsequently apologised for.

Misery again swamped her. Her own growing attraction to him had to be extinguished, and quickly. Maybe she should leave, after all. Out of sight, out of mind, and all that. But who'd care for Jamie?

She went up the stairs to her room, still agonising over her dilemma. She needed a distraction. As if someone had heard her, her own mobile rang. It was Rosie.

'Oh, am I glad to hear you.'

'What's wrong?'

'Th-that woman — Cassie,' Kathryn burst out. 'She just rang, wanting to speak to Sebastian. She's so rude, so arrogant. She's utterly, utterly detestable.'

'My, my, calm down, dear,' she light-heartedly told Kathryn. 'But I have to agree, I thought she was rude too. So what did she want him for?'

Rosie sounded very interested, Kathryn decided. 'They were supposed to meet for lunch and Sebastian was late, very late.'

'Are they an item then, as I thought?'

'I've no idea and I couldn't care less.'

'I see.' There was a pause, then, 'Do you want to meet up this evening for a drink?'

'Oh yes, please. Anything to get out of this house.'

Which was why she was walking into the Red Lion a bit later that same evening, her mood still one of extreme vexation.

Sebastian had finally arrived home at six thirty. Jamie and Olivia had returned from their walk a couple of hours before that and Olivia had retired to her room, pleading complete exhaustion. In fact she did look tired, so Joyce took her up a tray of tea.

Jamie had had his meal and he was undressed and ready for bed when Sebastian strode in. He too looked tired, strained even; his eyes were shadowed and heavy. Kathryn wondered if he and Cassie had had a row over his lateness.

'Cassie phoned,' she told him.

'Yes, I know. I was delayed at my previous meeting.'

That didn't sound as if his and Cassie's meeting was of a romantic nature; it sounded more like a business meeting. For a second her spirits lifted, only to sink back down as she realised he'd hardly let her know what sort of meeting it was. As Cassie had pointed out, she was only the nanny, albeit a temporary one.

Jamie was dancing around his father's legs. 'You put me to bed, Daddy. Kathryn's going out.'

Sebastian's sideways glance was a questioning one. 'Oh?'

'I'm meeting a friend, but I'd intended putting Jamie to bed first. That is why I'm here, after all; why you're paying me,' she coolly retorted. Sebastian eyed her, his expression a strange combination of suspicion and anticipation.

He was waiting for her to say who she was meeting. Well, he was destined for disappointment. She had no intention of revealing that it was Rosie. It was none of his business what she did in her own time. She was just the nanny, after all.

'Right. Well, if you want to get off, I'll deal with Jamie.' Although his tone matched hers in coolness now, he did allow his gaze to linger on her for a few heart-wrenching seconds before looking down at his son. 'So come on, fella, let's go.' And he swung the little boy up into his arms.

Kathryn felt her heart melt then. Whatever else he might be, he was an excellent father.

'Oh, by the way, where's my mother?'

'Granny's exhausted. She's gone to bed,' Jamie told him. 'She said I'm a real live wire. What's that, Daddy? Is it like a telegraph wire?'

Sebastian laughed and hugged his son. 'Something like that. Come on and tell me which story you want.' He swivelled his head to look back at Kathryn. 'Have a good evening.'

But as well-meaning as his words sounded, there was an expression in his eyes that didn't quite bear out that sentiment. Kathryn was tempted to come clean, right there and then, and admit it was only Rosie she was meeting. But something, some sort of stubborn sense of self-preservation, stopped her. After all, he'd just spent the better part of the afternoon with his — what? Girlfriend? Intended fiancée? Although maybe by now she was indeed his fiancée. Perhaps he'd heeded his mother's remarks and popped the question. In which case, let him go on wondering what she was up to — if that was what he was indeed doing. Which he probably wasn't. Why should he, when he was clearly in love with Cassie? Her activities would have no interest for him whatsoever.

An ache started up in her chest. For heaven's sake, she told herself, she was supposed to be quashing any feelings for him. Instead of which, she was causing herself more pain with her futile imaginings.

10

'So come on, what gives with you and Sebastian? And what were you so irate about? Just 'cause he's meeting someone else?'

'I'm not irate. Well I am, a bit. It's her and the way she talks to me. I feel an inch high.'

Rosie narrowed her eyes at her. 'Hmmm. You're not falling for him, are you? Because all of this sounds remarkably like jealousy to me.'

'Me? Jealous?' Kathryn cried. She wasn't about to admit that that was exactly what she was — not even to her best friend. 'No, I'm just worried, if they do make a go of it, about Jamie.'

'Jamie?' Rosie looked thoroughly confused now.

'Yeah. Cassie is definitely not mother material.'

'My God! It's that serious, is it?'

'It's beginning to sound like it.'

'Well I have to admit, he is seriously gorgeous.' Rosie wasn't quite smacking her lips. 'I wouldn't mind finding out whether I could get something going with him. It might stop him from marrying what's-her-name. Although — ' She tilted her head to one side. ' — do I want a ready-made family?'

'Rosie!'

'Well as I said, he is gorgeous and rich — stinking rich, in fact, from what I've heard.'

'For goodness sake,' Kathryn muttered.

'Maybe I ought to give what's-her-name — '

'Cassie,' Kathryn impatiently put in.

'Yeah, her — give her a run for her money. Y'know, make a play for him. Might be fun — and if I succeed it might even do her a bit of good not to have things all her own way. Because she strikes me as being one very spoilt lady.'

Even though Kathryn knew that

Rosie was only joking, she still experienced a sharp stabbing pain in the region of her heart at the notion of her friend and Sebastian together.

'Would you mind if I did? There's no one else on the scene as far as I'm concerned at the moment.'

It took some seconds for Kathryn to realise that Rosie meant it.

'Um — ' Kathryn swallowed the words of protest that sprang out of nowhere, and instead said, 'No, goodness, why should I mind?' She attempted a careless laugh, but made the mistake of picking up her glass and taking a large gulp of wine all at the same time. Of course, the inevitable happened. It went down the wrong way and she began to choke and splutter as she fought frantically for breath.

'That upsetting, huh?' Rosie said, energetically thumping her on the back.

As Kathryn slowly recovered her breath, Rosie quietly said, 'You're falling for him, aren't you? Big time.'

It was no good trying to pretend indifference any longer. Rosie had known her too long; she'd see through any protest she might make in a second. She nodded. 'I've tried so hard not to, but the feelings simply won't go away. Oh Rosie.' Hot tears stung her eyes. 'What am I going to do?'

'You're sure he doesn't feel the same about you?'

'One hundred percent sure.'

But was she? Sometimes she caught a certain expression in Sebastian's eye. And then there were those kisses. For a man who she presumed was indifferent to her, they'd been very passionate, very passionate indeed. Could she be wrong in thinking he didn't feel the same way she did?

No, of course he didn't; it was wishful thinking on her part. She wasn't his type. She was merely someone to amuse himself with when there was no one else available. Cassie was much more the sort of woman he'd be happy with: worldly; sophisticated, sure of her own place in the scheme of things. Yet look at how he'd reacted to Jack's display of interest in her, as well as her supposed interest in Jack — or was that nothing more than wishful thinking, too? Had he simply been angry that two people whom he employed had been enjoying a flirtation on his time? She sighed.

She eventually left Rosie and drove back to Willow Court. The house was in darkness, to her relief, except for the customary light left on in the hall. She usually turned it off if she'd been out. She quietly unlocked the front door and stepped inside. Equally quietly, she closed it behind her again, locking it securely before turning and heading on tip toes for the stairs.

'Kathryn?'

She whirled round, her breath catching in her throat as she saw Sebastian, his one shoulder propped against the door jamb of the sitting room, his legs crossed at the ankles, his gaze a bleak one. His arms were also crossed.

'Oh, I-I thought everyone was in bed. Sorry, did I disturb you?'

'You could say that. I've been waiting for you.'

'You have? Why?'

'Why?' He echoed her tone. 'Why do you think?'

'I-I've no idea.'

He pulled away from the doorway and strode towards her, his expression a dark one. 'Who have you been with? Jack? The ex? Who?'

'Neither. Anyway, Matt's back in Dubai.'

'So — ' His gaze hadn't left her throughout all of this. ' — someone new then?'

'N-no,' she stammered.

'Not another old boyfriend? How many do you have, for God's sake?'

'Why are you so interested in who I've been with?'

'Why do you think?' His eyes narrowed as he moved closer; he looked dangerous all of a sudden. She took a step back, but it was nowhere near enough. For he simply reached out and grabbed her by the arm.

'I-I really don't know,' she gasped.

'Well, I'll tell you. Because of this, that's why.' And he yanked her into him, their chests colliding hard as he slid one arm about her waist; he then cupped her chin, tilting her face up to his.

'Wh-what are you doing?' she stammered.

He didn't answer. And no wonder. It was perfectly obvious what he was doing. He lowered his head to hers and laid claim to her lips.

As always happened the moment he touched her, Kathryn was powerless to move, let alone summon up the ability to protest. His kiss literally took her breath away. It was passionate, searching, demanding. It moved down over her arched throat, on down to the cleft between her breasts. His hands began to trace her curves as every one of her nerve endings began to throb. Kathryn felt herself respond, just like she had before, completely helpless against her overwhelming need for him, as her insides turned to molten liquid and her legs threatened to give way beneath her. Lord help her, she was in love with him — totally, desperately.

But then Cassie's lovely face swam before her and with an anguished cry she broke free and pushed him away. 'How could you?'

'Oh my God.' He stared at her, his face drained of blood. 'Kathryn — '

But Kathryn didn't wait to hear any more. An apology simply wouldn't do, not this time. She'd already thought he was amusing himself with her while saving his love for someone else, and she, fool that she was, kept letting him.

She bolted for the stairs, desperate to get away before she revealed exactly how she felt.

* * *

It wasn't until she'd closed her bedroom door behind her that she gave way to her emotions. She threw herself across the bed and let the tears flow.

Just as she'd feared she would, she'd fallen in love. Deeply, irrevocably in love.

And what about Sebastian? What had he been thinking? That because she worked for him he could do just as he wanted? Marry Cassie, but keep Kathryn on the sidelines — purely for the odd spot of dalliance? It was medieval; the sort of thing an ancient lord of the manor would do. She would never have believed it of him, never. Because if what she'd overheard between his mother and him was anything to go by, he was literally on the verge of telling Cassie that he loved her. It had to be Cassie. Who else could it be? It couldn't be her, Kathryn, because as she repeatedly told herself, she wasn't his type. But the doubts crowded in once more. If she was his type and it was her he truly wanted, why didn't he tell her?

Her heart ached as she realised what an impossible situation she was in. Perhaps a night's sleep would help her to see it all in a clearer light

— providing she could sleep, that was.

But morning brought no answers with it. It also didn't help that Olivia came to say goodbye.

'As much as I'd love to stay a bit longer, I really do have to get back. I've got a couple of appointments that I simply can't miss.'

'Oh, I'm sorry.' Kathryn liked Sebastian's mother and having her there would help alleviate any strain between her son and Kathryn.

'Get Sebastian to bring you to Cornwall some time,' the older woman went on. 'Not in August; it's far too busy then. It's lovely in September.'

'Well as I said, I don't expect to be working for him much longer.'

'Oh, I wouldn't bet on that,' Olivia murmured, almost beneath her breath. 'Jamie is very fond of you.'

Yes, thought Kathryn, he was. If only Sebastian felt the same way. But the truth was she hadn't a clue as to how Sebastian felt about her, other than someone he could kiss whenever he felt so inclined — in between his lovemaking with Cassie, of course.

* * *

But it was the next morning that things became horribly clear. She was playing with Jamie, helping him race his toy cars, of which he had an extensive collection, around the hallway.

'Come on, Kathryn,' he chuckled, 'I'm beating you.'

'I know you are.'

'Look, this is how you do it.' He literally flung the car he was holding. It leapt through the air, landing hard, to then slide several feet before disappearing beneath a large oak bureau which stood against one wall.

'Oh no!' he shouted. 'I've lost it! It's my favourite.' His bottom lip began to quiver.

'Don't worry, darling,' Kathryn soothed him. 'I'm sure I can reach underneath and find it.'

The bureau stood on short legs, with

a gap between it and the floor of a mere four inches. Kathryn lay flat on her stomach; it was the only way to reach underneath. She stretched an arm out and groped around. She couldn't find the car, but her hand touched something. It was right at the back, against the wall. She managed to grasp it and pulled it out. It was a scrunched-up piece of paper.

'That's not my car!' Jamie cried. 'Get my car.'

'Okay, okay, hold on to your horses, my lad.'

'I haven't got any horses,' Jamie crossly said. 'Silly Kathryn.'

With a grin, Kathryn reached under the bureau again and this time located the small car. She dragged it out. 'There — success.' She got to her feet and, after quickly brushing off the cobwebs and dust that had clung to it, she handed it to him. Clearly, Joyce's cleaning didn't extend to the undersides of certain pieces of furniture.

'Thanks, Kathryn,' he beamed, and

returned once more to his car racing. Kathryn unfolded the piece of paper, smoothing it out with her fingers, wiping off the dust and cobwebs from that too as she did so. It was a letter; a letter to Sara.

She started to fold it up, intending to ask Joyce what she should do with it — she was loath to give it to Sebastian in case it caused him undue distress to have a letter written to his dead wife — when she spotted the signature at the bottom. Cassandra.

Cassandra? Why was Cassandra writing to Sara?

She glanced at the top again. It wasn't dated. She could only assume it had been written before Sara's death. She couldn't help herself; she began to read it.

11

Sara —

I think you should know that Sebastian and I are very much in love and have been for some time. The truth is he no longer wants you; he wants me. He's planning to leave you and marry me. So the best thing you can do — for everyone — is to go first. I'm telling you this with the best of intentions, Cassandra

Kathryn's hand, the hand that was holding the letter, began to shake as the significance of the words she'd read began to sink in.

Oh God. She could just have discovered the reason for Sara's suicide. Oh, dear God. She all but fell onto the nearby chair. What should she do?

'Kathryn, what's wrong?' It was Jamie. He'd looked up from his play and was now staring anxiously at her. 'What's that?' He pointed to the letter.

Kathryn quickly folded it up and slipped it into her jeans pocket. 'Oh, nothing, darling. It's nothing.'

Rosie and Matt had both been right: Sebastian and Cassie between them had driven Sara to kill herself. Did Sebastian know about the letter? Had he encouraged Cassie to write it? Condoned it, even? But they couldn't have foreseen the tragic consequences, surely?

She felt sick. What should she do with the letter? Give it to Sebastian? Sara must have been so horrified to receive it that she'd scrunched it up and thrown it from her. It had ended up beneath the bureau to lie undiscovered all this time. It was the only explanation.

'Kathryn, come on. Let's play some more.'

Somehow, and she didn't know how, Kathryn managed to enter into the spirit of the game again. And all the while, the note burnt a hole in her pocket. In the end, she didn't show it to anyone.

She hid it right at the back of a drawer in her bedroom and tried to forget about it. Tried to forget that the man she had so foolishly and fruitlessly fallen in love with had, with the help of his lover, most probably driven his wife to take her own life.

* * *

The next couple of days passed in a blur of agonising indecision for Kathryn. Not only about whether to give the note to Sebastian, but also about whether she should stay or leave. If he had known about the letter, what did that make him? And how could she go on working for such a callous man?

She saw practically nothing of him, other than for when he gave her his instructions for the work he wanted her to do — for which she was truly thankful. She didn't know, in the light of what she now suspected, how she should behave with him, or whether she'd have the stomach to even speak to him. And, if he was in love with Cassie, which if the words in the letter were to be believed he was, and his intention was to marry her, why hadn't he done so? What was he waiting for? And why had he kissed her, Kathryn? Not once but several times. As she'd already asked herself, several times, was he simply amusing himself with her? Toying with her emotions? Has he guessed she loved him and so was taking unscrupulous advantage of that?

Whatever his reason, he was despicable. But no matter how often she told herself that, she still couldn't seem to stop loving him.

She kept herself busy by taking Jamie on long walks — well, as long as his little legs would allow, and having riding lessons with Jed. He proved to be a good teacher: patient, understanding.

'You're a natural rider, Kathryn,' he told her. 'Maybe you should ask Mr Grant to buy a horse for you.'

'Oh, I won't be staying here, Jed.'

'Won't you?' He regarded her with

astonishment. 'I thought — '

'What?'

'Nothing, nothing at all. I obviously misunderstood.' And he wouldn't be drawn any further.

But if Jed had believed she was a fixture at Willow Court, she couldn't let Jamie think the same. So when he asked, 'Are you going to stay with me forever, Kathryn?' she immediately said, 'No, I can't do that, darling.'

'Why not?' he fretfully demanded.

'Because I have another job to do.'

He stuck out his lower lip. 'But Granny said you'd be ideal — if only Daddy would see what was right under his nose. I heard her.'

Kathryn was lost for words. However, that didn't stop her heart aching, both for herself and this small boy standing in front of her, beseeching her.

'Why can't you stay?' Jamie's bottom lip was beginning to quiver now. 'I want you to stay.'

'Oh Jamie, sweetheart, I'm only here temporarily.'

'What's tem-temprally?'

'Just for a short while, until Daddy finds you a proper nanny, and that's not me.'

'Yes it is!' he shouted.

Kathryn couldn't help but smile. But the conversation disturbed her deeply. Jamie was the one who was going to be most hurt when the time came for her to leave. Maybe she should find out whether Sebastian was actually doing anything about finding a replacement for her. Or was he thinking that once he and Cassie were married he wouldn't need to find another nanny? Again, she wondered why they just didn't get on with it. There was nothing stopping them.

* * *

The following Sunday, Kathryn felt she wanted a break from Willow Court and its inhabitants, so once again she went home. She needed some time to reassess her situation and try and decide what she should do.

She let herself in and almost at once heard the sound of voices coming from the kitchen. Raised voices.

'How could they do this to me?' This was Jess.

Kathryn was sorely tempted to turn around and silently let herself out again. What had happened now? The last thing she needed was Jess ranting and raving. Could Fitz have ended things between them?

She went into the kitchen. Jess whirled to face her. 'Oh, it's you. Just the person I wanted to see.'

Kathryn's heart sank. 'Me? Why?'

'Your — boss has made me redundant.'

'Oh no. When?' Her heart sank even lower.

'I had the letter yesterday.' Jess waved a sheet of paper at her. 'You'll have to talk to him. I need my job.'

'Jess, I can't talk to him. It's nothing to do with me.'

'Well, you could at least try.'

'No, I couldn't.'

'Well, thank you very much!' Jess turned and literally stormed from the kitchen.

'Dad — ' Kathryn looked at her father. ' — what about you? Have you received a redundancy notice?'

'No, it's just the people who have been most recently taken on, people like Jess. She'll calm down.'

Kathryn looked at her mother. Helen looked troubled. 'Mum?'

'Oh Kathryn, couldn't you try to talk to him?'

'No, Mum, I can't. He'd probably tell me to mind my own business in any case, the mood he's in.'

'Oh dear. Things not going well?'

'It's not that.' But Kathryn could feel the stirrings of anger with Sebastian. Didn't he realise what a huge thing it was for people to lose their job? Was he so far removed from everyone lower down the scale? He, who had so much? 'Okay, I'll try and talk to him but I don't know if he'll listen.' A man who could treat the woman who cared for his son so heartlessly was hardly likely to care about a lowly employee in a factory.

'Thank you, darling. Now, do you want a sherry?'

* * *

Next morning, after Sebastian had finished listing the tasks that he wanted her to do, she nerved herself to say, 'Um — I went home yesterday and — ' She swallowed nervously. How could she ask him to reinstate Jess when there were probably several others just as unfortunate, and just as deserving of their jobs? He'd refuse, for sure.

'Yes, and — ?' He was leafing through some papers and not looking at her. However, at her silence, he glanced up. 'Well, what is it? Is it Jamie?' He frowned anxiously.

'No, it's not Jamie. It's Jess.'

'Jess?' He looked puzzled now.

'My sister.'

'What about her?' He lowered his

gaze to the papers again.

'You-you've made her redundant.'

His head jerked up at that. 'Have I?'

'Yes. She heard on Saturday.'

'I see. Well yes, several employees have had to be let go.'

'Let go?' She could hear her voice rising. That was one way of saying he'd given her the sack.

'Kathryn, these things happen. The majority of the workforce — the greater majority, as it happens — will keep their jobs. It's unfortunate in Jess's case but — '

'But?'

'If it saves the jobs of all the others . . . ' He shrugged, as if the whole thing had very little to do with him.

Determined not to let him off the hook that easily, she went on. 'I see. So it's no good appealing to your better side.' She only just stopped herself from adding, 'That's supposing you've got one.' She didn't quite have the courage for that.

As if he'd read her thoughts, his

expression hardened. 'No, I'm sorry, but the decision's been made.'

'Right.' She swallowed the bitterness welling inside of her. She'd had the futile hope that because it was her asking, he'd have made an exception and agreed. How wrong could she have been? He cared nothing either for her or her family. 'So, in that case, have you done anything more about finding someone to look after Jamie?'

His gaze swept over her once again. 'I've had no luck at all, I'm afraid. Why? Is it a problem for you to stay?'

'Well, not as such, but Jamie is growing a little too attached to me. It'll make it very hard for him when I do have to go. I thought it should perhaps be soon.'

'Well, I haven't found anyone.' And yet again he shrugged, as if the matter wasn't really his concern.

Kathryn felt her anger flare. He was behaving as if her needs — and, more importantly, Jamie's — were insignificant; trivial, even. 'I do have a life, you know, outside of this house, and I'd really like to resume it,' she snapped.

'I'm sure you would.' His tone, as well as his stare, had cooled even more in the wake of her bad temper. 'But what can I do? I can't hire just anyone. Surely you wouldn't want me to do that. To place Jamie in the care of someone incompetent? And if this is some sort of retaliation for your sister's redundancy — ?'

She took a deep breath, fighting for calm. How dare he? The fury rose, black and hot. He actually thought she'd use Jamie as some sort of bargaining tool; a threat to hold over him.

'It's not. And if you're implying that-that I'd use Jamie to-to get you to reinstate Jess — ' Words failed her, so great was her sense of outrage; of injustice.

'I'm not, not really,' he went on. 'I'm sure you wouldn't go to those lengths, would you?' His glance was a searching one now.

'No, but I do have to think about

finding another job.'

'Why? Don't I pay you enough? I'll increase your wage.'

'No, no,' she cried, 'it's not that at all. It's — well, I'm not a qualified nanny.'

'You seem rather good at it to me,' he murmured. 'Born to do it, actually.'

She was getting nowhere with this. Why had Jess and her mother thought she'd have any influence over this man? He was a law unto himself.

'You obviously need a break. I was thinking of going down to Provence — France, you know?' His glance now was a quizzical one.

'Yes, I do know where Provence is,' she muttered.

'I have a villa there about fifteen minutes from Nice. I've invited some friends to join me. I think you and Jamie should come too.'

Oh you do, do you? was her silent response. Just like that? No, 'Would you like to come?' Just, 'I think you should come.' She had her mouth open to say, 'No, thank you,' when he demanded,

'You do have a passport, I take it?'

'Of course.'

'That's settled then. We go on Monday and stay for a week.'

Kathryn gave up. What was the point in arguing? There was just one question that niggled at her. Was Cassie going to be there?

Yes, was the most likely answer to that. If friends were joining him, he'd hardly leave the woman he loved behind, would he?

12

The next few days flew by and all the while Kathryn battled with her inner self. One minute she'd decide she wouldn't go to Provence, the next she would; a holiday might do her good, she'd tell herself, only to conclude that spending the entire week in Sebastian's company would, unarguably, be the most foolish thing she'd ever done. Dangerous, even. And so she went on, arguing the case back and forth, back and forth, until her head literally whirled.

And throughout it all, she repeatedly asked herself, how could she love a man who showed so little regard for anyone else? Being with him in such close and uninterrupted proximity, even for just a week, would simply cause her added heartache and anguish, especially now she knew that he and Cassandra had been having an affair while Sara was still alive. On the other hand, though, it might help her to put things back into perspective; show her that Sebastian simply wasn't worth loving.

The end result of all of this was that by the time they left for the airport, she felt wrung out and exhausted with her indecision. Still, finally they were on their way, and it was too late to back out. It was almost a relief.

Jamie, not surprisingly, was beside himself with excitement.

'What will we do when we get there, Kathryn?' he repeatedly asked.

'Have fun,' she answered, hoping against hope that would prove true and that she wouldn't regret her decision to go.

They arrived in Nice beneath a cloudless blue sky to encounter the sort of heat that was practically suffocating. Kathryn followed Sebastian from the airport terminal to the car that he'd arranged to have waiting for them. So far there'd been no sign of either Cassie or the friends who were supposedly joining them. In fact, she'd been surprised that Cassie hadn't travelled with them. Presumably they'd all be arriving on another flight? Her heart sank at the prospect.

But if Kathryn was apprehensive, Jamie was a tinderbox of anticipation. He'd never flown before and every second that passed had been filled with wonder and delight for him. He'd chattered non-stop all the way.

It had been almost as exciting for Kathryn, although she'd managed to still her tongue except for the occasional response to a remark of Sebastian's. She'd felt his gaze upon her, however, more often than had been comfortable. He'd looked to be deriving a great deal of pleasure from both her and his son's highly visible enjoyment of everything. For the truth was she'd never flown first class anywhere, or had an air-conditioned car complete with driver waiting to transport her to her destination. Sebastian clearly didn't believe in stinting himself.

Mind you, he probably wouldn't be allowed to if he married Cassie.

The villa when they reached it literally put the icing on an already exotic cake and took Kathryn's breath away. She gasped at the sight of the whitewashed walls, smothered in magenta bougainvillaea rambling beneath a terracotta roof. French windows led out onto shady terraces, and on the first floor there were wrought-iron balconies everywhere she looked. A gravelled forecourt stretched the entire length of the house and as the car scrunched to a halt, the front door opened and a stocky, smiling woman rushed out.

'M'sieur Grant,' she beamed, 'it ees so good to see you again. And Jamie. You 'ave grown; you are a leetle man now.' And without further ado, she pulled him into her ample bosom — much to Jamie's dismay, if the expression upon his small face was anything to go by. 'You and I will 'ave such fun.' She then glanced up at Sebastian. 'You need 'ave no worries. As I said last time you were

’ere, I will take care of ’im.’ Her glance then slid to Kathryn and for a second complete bewilderment filled her eyes. ‘Uh — Madame Grant?’

‘Oh no,’ Kathryn rushed to contradict her. ‘I take care of Jamie. I’m Kathryn Kirkwood.’

The woman’s expression of disappointment was almost comical. All Kathryn could think was, why had Sebastian been so keen for her to come, if this affable woman was so keen to care for Jamie? Maybe, as he’d said, he really had thought it would do her good — or, much more likely, she waspishly reflected, persuade her to stay. After all, as she’d already concluded more than once now, it wouldn’t suit him to have her leave before he’d found someone else, Cassie or no Cassie. Treating her to a luxury holiday could be his way of ensuring she remained, instead of the magnanimous gesture it seemed.

‘You will have more than enough to do taking care of all of us, without having to run round after Jamie,’

Sebastian smoothly put in.

'As you wish, M'sieur Grant.'

Sebastian then turned to Kathryn, his glance moving immediately to her flushed cheeks. The gleam in his eye told her that he was fully aware of her embarrassment at being mistaken for his wife. She dreaded to think how Cassie would have reacted if she'd been there. It would most likely have been the excuse for yet more venom. 'This is Maria, Kathryn, who looks after the villa for me. I don't know what I would do without her.'

'Oh, M'sieur Grant,' she simpered. For heaven's sake, Kathryn irritably reflected, the woman was all but curtseying to him. 'You are too kind.'

'Not at all,' Sebastian politely riposted. 'It's perfectly true.'

'Come, Mees Kirkwood, I will show you to your room. It was a leetle short notice but . . . ' Her tone contained a barb of criticism — not for Sebastian, it seemed to Kathryn, but for her. She felt a stab of irritation. It wasn't her fault that Sebastian hadn't warned the woman in good time that she would be an addition to the party. She was beginning to wish she had turned the invitation down. 'But I 'ave everything ready for you all,' Maria finished.

'Thank you, Maria. I knew I could rely on you.' Sebastian bestowed an especially warm smile upon her.

This time Maria really did bob a curtsey. Good grief! No wonder Sebastian had such an inflated idea of his own importance. Even Joyce practically worshipped him, although Kathryn had never seen her actually curtsey to him.

'If you will follow me, Mees Kirkwood — and Jamie,' Maria invited, holding out a hand to the small boy, who had been standing silent throughout all of this, eyes like saucers, taking everything in.

'Oh please, call me Kathryn,' Kathryn invited. 'It's easier.'

'Thank you, I will. Will you come this way?' Without further ado, she swung to lead the way out of the large hallway and up the stairs.

'Kathryn,' Jamie whispered, turning to look at her, 'why is she speaking in that funny voice?'

'Because she's French, darling,' Kathryn whispered back. 'Now go along with her. You don't want to hurt her feelings. And I'll come and collect you in five minutes.'

The bedroom that Kathryn was ushered into was another revelation. A king-sized bed sat against one wall, while built-in wardrobes and a vanity unit all but filled another. A door at the end of these led into an aquamarine-and-ivory marbled bathroom, and a third wall was constructed entirely of glass, with sliding doors leading out onto a balcony identical to the ones that she'd seen upon arrival, complete with two chairs and a table as well as a cushioned recliner. This balcony, however, instead of looking out over the forecourt, had a view down onto a shimmering turquoise swimming pool and a sprawling garden of cream-coloured gravel, liberally freckled with dozens of succulent plants and palm trees as well as more of the ubiquitous bougainvillea. She could even see the blue of the Mediterranean.

It didn't take her long to unpack her clothes. She swiftly removed the things she'd travelled in to slip on a strappy top over a pair of just-above-the-knee white shorts; beneath this she wore a bikini. She wasn't quite sure what was expected of her but her outfit should cover most things. She then went to Jamie's room next door to hers and dressed the little boy in swimming trunks and a T-shirt. Maria had unpacked his case, she saw.

'Can we swim, Kathryn?' he excitedly asked, hopping from one foot to another.

'I should think so. Just a quick one, though. I don't know what Daddy's plans are. Here, let's put on your inflatable arm bands.'

Within a matter of minutes they were splashing happily in the gloriously warm water of the Olympic-sized pool

— just the two of them, to Kathryn's relief. Her bikini was fairly skimpy. Unfortunately she only possessed more of the same, so she'd have to try and ignore Sebastian's gleaming gaze.

But for now Kathryn watched Jamie doggy paddling across the pool. She stretched her arms over her head, glorying in the warmth and the sensation of the water on her over-heated body as finally she sank down into it. The air around them was scented. It must be from the abundance of flowers and plants that surrounded the villa.

Two girls came out of the house and began to lay the large table that sat on the terrace nearest to the pool. It was shaded by a pergola literally dripping with a massive vine. They were laying it for three people, so clearly the other guests weren't expected yet. She hadn't asked who they would be, for fear that Sebastian would confirm her worst fear, that Cassie was indeed coming. She didn't want these first few enjoyable hours spoiled. She'd face that unpleasantness when it happened. As it surely would.

She turned her attention back to Jamie, still happily splashing in the shallow end, so she didn't notice Sebastian come out through the French windows and approach the pool. The first she knew of his presence was the sound of him diving into the water.

'Daddy, Daddy!' Jamie shrieked. 'Look, I'm swimming!' He proceeded to execute a series of rapid arm movements, propelling himself towards his father. When he reached Sebastian he clutched at him, gasping and spitting water from his mouth.

'I can see that,' Sebastian laughed as he picked his son up and tossed him into the air, to catch him again right before he hit the water. Jamie screamed with delight, making Kathryn laugh too as she stood upright to watch father and son cavorting together.

Too late, she became aware of Sebastian's gaze as it took its time roaming over her, lingering a little too long on the generous amount of cleavage that her bikini revealed. In desperation, she ducked down beneath the water again. She'd have to try and buy something that provided more cover than the bikini did. Maybe a one-piece costume?

She stared back at him, silently daring him to comment, but all he did was to lift one eyebrow and allow his mouth to twist with the merest hint of a grin. Really, the man was impossible. Here he was, on the verge of marrying one woman, and unabashedly flirting with another. Had he got no principles? Huh! Stupid question. Of course he hadn't, not if he'd been carrying on with Cassie while married to Sara. Had she been forced to stand by and watch his lecherous behaviour? If she had, it was no wonder she'd been in such despair.

'If you want a proper swim,' he called, 'I'll stay with Jamie.'

'Thanks, I will if you don't mind.'

'I don't. Go ahead, then we'll have lunch, okay?'

'Fine.' And she was gone, expertly swimming towards the deep end, her body streaking through the water, acutely aware of Sebastian's keen-eyed gaze following her every inch of the way.

Lunch was delicious: salad Niçoise followed, as was the French custom, by a selection of ripe cheeses, before finishing with a freshly made Mediterranean fruit salad. Throughout the entire meal Jamie chattered nonstop, something for which Kathryn felt only gratitude. The atmosphere between her and Sebastian remained strained.

At long last, and more for something to say rather than to discover whether Cassie was coming or not, she asked, 'When do you expect your other guests to arrive?' Only to be interrupted by the excited babble of several voices.

'Sebastian, darling, we're here — finally.'

Cassie; she'd know that voice anywhere.

Dismay all but crushed Kathryn in

that second. She'd been so hoping she wouldn't be coming. Sebastian must know how much she disliked Cassie and how much Cassie disliked her. He'd have to be blind and totally insensitive not to. So why would he invite them both? It was hardly likely to result in a relaxing holiday for any of them.

Sebastian had risen to his feet before striding to the open French doors to greet his guests as they arrived.

'There you are. Oh no, are we too late for lunch? I'm ravenous.'

This was said by a woman whom Kathryn didn't know. A friend of Cassie's? She was even more lovely than Cassie was: shoulder-length, honey-blonde, silky smooth hair; eyes the exact shade of bluebells; a pair of lips that looked ready-made for kissing, and a figure to die for. That was on full show with the aid of a low-cut, tight-fitting, short-skirted dress. Kathryn didn't know why she'd worried about the brevity of her bikini. There was no way Sebastian would waste time looking at her with both Cassie and this vision parading in front of him.

Kathryn stumbled to her feet just as Jamie, too, scrambled down from the table, running towards the woman, crying, 'Auntie Lucy — it's me. I'm here.'

'Oh, my word. Who is this grown-up young man?' And the woman — Lucy, obviously — bent down to swing Jamie up into her arms. He didn't even glance at Cassie, Kathryn noticed. Evidently he didn't care for her any more than Kathryn did. A pang of compassion for the small boy pierced her. How was he going to react to her becoming his step-mother?

As for Cassie, she looked every bit as displeased to see Kathryn as Kathryn had been to see her. 'Oh, it's you.' She then swung to Sebastian. 'You didn't say you were bringing the nanny when we spoke a couple of days ago. This is all very last-minute, isn't it? Lovely surprise, though, but I've barely had time to get my nails done, let alone the rest of the preparations that a visit to

Provence entails.'

Kathryn was puzzled. Sebastian had given her the impression that this week had been planned before he'd mentioned her coming along. Now it was sounding as if he'd organised it on the spur of the moment after he'd invited her. Once again, she wondered if it was a deliberate ploy to get her to remain as Jamie's nanny — a practical demonstration of the luxurious benefits of staying.

Cassie, running true to form, immediately turned her back on Kathryn, deliberately excluding her from the group. There were five people in all: Cassie and Lucy, plus two men and then, of course, Sebastian. Sebastian now turned to draw Kathryn into the circle. 'Kathryn, let me introduce you. Cassie, you know; and Lucy, who is married to Daniel.' He indicated one of the men, who smiled warmly at Kathryn, and mouthed 'hello'. 'Lucy and I have been friends for years. We try and get together a couple of times a year. The last member of the group is

Robert Wells. Robert is one of my best and most valued associates, as well as a good friend.'

Her heart sank so low she fully expected to see it oozing from between her toes. Sebastian must be hoping she and Robert would pair up. Otherwise, why invite an extra man? Oh Lord, that could be embarrassing. Robert, she was sure, was a very nice man, but absolutely not her type. He was of medium height, stockily built, with receding brown hair that was already greying. She'd put his age at somewhere between forty-five and fifty. What had Sebastian been thinking? That she had a thing for older men?

'Cassie, you know your way.'

Cassie had been here with him before, then. Well of course she had, if they were as close as the letter suggested. They probably shared a room. She wouldn't think about that — couldn't bear to, as a matter of fact. Why, oh why, she agonised, had she agreed to come? And more to the point, why had Sebastian insisted she did? He had no need of her. He had Maria, who clearly had been eager to take charge of the small boy. He must have thought she needed a holiday. But that would suggest he was a caring, sensitive man who, if he'd known about Cassie's letter, was complicit in the sending of it. In fact, he quite evidently wasn't. It didn't make sense.

'You're in the lemon room, Robert. I'll get Maria to show you to yours. Lucy and Daniel, you're in the rose room. You two know your way.'

Maria appeared then with a man whom Kathryn hadn't seen before.

'Ah, Gaston — Maria's husband for anyone who doesn't know. Would you like to take the baggage up for my guests?'

'I'll see you later, Sebastian,' Cassie said, daintily fluttering her fingers at him. 'I must have a shower and a little rest. Too, too hot.' She once more waved her fingers, this time including almost everyone in her goodbye, except for Kathryn, that was. She totally ignored Kathryn.

'I'll put Jamie down for a rest too,' Kathryn said to Sebastian, 'until the heat subsides a little. We don't want him to get sunburnt.'

'No, no!' Jamie cried. 'I want another swim. Daddy — ple-ease.'

'Later, sweetheart,' his father said. 'You don't swim right after a meal. Do as Kathryn says.'

'You didn't mention that Cassie would be here,' Kathryn couldn't resist blurting.

Sebastian swivelled his head to look straight at her. 'Is that a problem?'

She shrugged. 'Not as such, but I don't think she approves of mixing socially with the help,' she bluntly concluded.

'Oh, take no notice of Cassie. She's like that with everyone.'

'She's not like it with you, or Lucy and Daniel, or with Robert, either,' she bit back. 'She's great pals with you all.'

He eyed Kathryn, a hard glint

appearing within his eye. 'I rather hoped this week together would give you an opportunity to get to know each other a little better.'

'Did you?' Should she tell him hell would have time to freeze over before she and Cassie became friends?

'Yes, but I'll have a word with her.'

'Oh, please, not on my account. I am only the nanny, after all. I'll just have to make sure I remember my place — in the background. Or maybe I should go stay with Maria and Gaston. Would that make everyone happy?' And, holding her head high, she stalked from the room, holding Jamie firmly by the hand.

'Kathryn,' Sebastian furiously began, 'you are not the nanny. You are my guest.'

But Kathryn wasn't listening. She was already halfway up the stairs, Jamie complaining bitterly at her side, 'You're going too fast, Kathryn. I'm only little.'

13

Kathryn didn't return to the pool. She, too, decided to have a rest. She went into her room, opened the windows wide onto the balcony and tried not to listen to the voices rising up towards her in the still air.

She could hear Sebastian. His voice was a distinctive one: smooth, velvety, almost; yet at the same time throaty, seductively so. Lucy, Daniel and Robert were with him and by the sounds that were coming up to her, they were splashing around in the water.

She undressed and lay on the bed in just her bikini. The air conditioning was on and the coolness gently and gradually soothed her until eventually, worn out by the day's events, she slept.

It was Jamie's voice that roused her in the end. 'Kathryn, Kathryn, I'm awake.'

She glanced at the clock on the

bedside table. It was five o'clock. She'd slept for almost two hours. 'Coming, sweetheart,' she called back.

The terrace was in shade by the time she and Jamie returned to the others. Everyone was present and drinks were already being served by Gaston.

'Glass of Pimms, Kathryn?' Sebastian asked.

'Yes, please.' She ignored Cassie's look of displeasure that she should be daring to join them. Obviously Sebastian hadn't said anything to her yet about her attitude towards Kathryn. She began to doubt whether he would. Why would he deliberately upset the woman he was in love with — and thus spoil his holiday with the inevitable row?

'Are you and Jamie joining us for dinner?' Cassie haughtily asked. 'Won't he be tired?'

'No. He's had a long sleep; he'll be fine.' She took the slim-line glass from the Frenchman, saying, 'Thank you, Gaston. That looks wonderful.'

'Cassie,' Sebastian said, 'just so that

things are crystal-clear. Kathryn is here as my guest, just as you are.'

Cassie looked genuinely astonished. 'Really? Do you always ask the nanny along as a guest?'

The other people around the table began to look uncomfortable and Lucy quickly broke in, 'So Kathryn, what do you normally do when you're not taking care of Jamie?'

Sebastian had seemingly told her that Kathryn's role was purely a temporary one and a wave of gratitude washed over her.

'I'm a PA — which, incidentally, I'm also acting as on a part-time basis for Sebastian.'

'Oh, really?' Cassie's expression altered to one of exasperated scorn.

'Yes, Sebastian's currently looking for a qualified nanny and as soon as he's found one, I'm off.' She didn't even glance his way as she said this, but she did note Lucy's slanting, slightly anxious glance at Sebastian.

'Well, I think he's rather hoping

you'll stay,' Lucy said quietly. Kathryn couldn't miss Cassie's snort to one side of her and her low mutter of 'I can't think why. Nannies are two a penny.'

'Maybe, but I wouldn't imagine that good PAs are,' was Lucy's curt response to this.

Cassie fell silent and conversation became more general.

Very soon, the candles that had been placed on the table were lit as the sun slowly set and dinner was served. Sebastian had disappeared inside to put a CD into the player and instantly music flooded onto the terrace, drowning out the strident chirruping of the cicadas that was coming from some nearby trees. It was Beethoven, Kathryn thought, although she was no expert on classical music. She glanced towards the pool; the water was illuminated by underwater lights, turning the blue into mauve, rose and gold. All in all, it was a charmingly romantic scene. It was just a pity it had to be spoiled by Cassie's spiteful attitude. But Kathryn could only suppose, as Sebastian's future wife, she assumed she had the right to act and speak as she wanted. Yet Kathryn still couldn't understand why they weren't already married. There'd been more than enough time — over two years, in fact.

As soon as dinner was over, Maria cleared the table and said softly to Sebastian, 'We'll leave as soon as the dishwasher ees loaded. But we'll be back to serve breakfast in the morning.'

'Thank you, Maria, and thank Gaston and your two young helpers. I very much appreciate what you do — all of you. Good night.'

'Good night, M'sieur.' She again dropped a small curtsey.

Cassie snorted, 'Now that's how servants should behave,' and she glared meaningfully at Kathryn.

Fortunately, the couple of glasses of wine that Kathryn had drunk on top of the Pimms had mellowed her sufficiently to enable her to ignore this further example of the other woman's snobbishness. However, she did catch Sebastian's muttered, 'For God's sake, Cassie, give it a rest. Kathryn's doing me a favour — I'll thank you to remember that.' To which Cassie made no response at all.

It soon became evident that Maria and Gaston's departure acted as some sort of signal. Cassie slipped inside and changed the CD to something romantic, turning up the volume to the wrong side of loud before coming back onto the terrace to stand in front of Sebastian and hold her arms out to him. Kathryn heard her throaty murmur quite clearly, as she began to swing her hips seductively from side to side. 'Dance with me, Sebastian.'

Time to go, Kathryn decided. She got to her feet, saying, 'Jamie, bedtime, I think. Say goodnight to everyone.'

Sebastian turned his head to look at her and said, 'Come back down, Kathryn, when you've got him settled,' before responding to Cassie's invitation.

'Oh well, I don't think . . . ' she

began to demur. She didn't know how much longer she could endure being treated as little more than a servant by Cassie. It had been hard enough for an evening. How would she survive a week of it?

'I insist,' he quietly said.

'Sebastian, if she doesn't want to, let her be,' Cassie spoke smugly. 'She's probably had a tough day running round after Jamie. He can be very energetic, not to say hyperactive,' she declared drily.

'He's been asleep all afternoon,' was Sebastian's tight-lipped reply to this. 'Kathryn, this is meant to be a holiday for you as well as us and I want you to enjoy yourself.'

'Okay.' It seemed easier to simply agree. He wasn't to know that she had other plans. And she really couldn't see him coming upstairs after her. She swung back to Jamie, who was doing the round of everyone, kissing them all good night — well, all except Cassie, that was. Lucy hugged him warmly, saying, 'Good night, little man. Sleep tight.'

It didn't take long to bathe him and get him into bed. He was tired after the excitement of the day. He put his arms around Kathryn's neck and whispered, 'I don't like Cassie, Kathryn. Why is she here?'

'Because Daddy asked her along.'

'I wish he hadn't. I wish it was just you, Daddy and me. I love you, Kathryn. I want you to stay.'

Kathryn felt her heart squeeze. Jamie was becoming far too attached to her.

'I want you to be my mummy.'

'Oh darling, I can't be that, but I do love you.' She kissed him and held him close. 'Now go to sleep, and I'll see you in the morning.'

He was asleep before she'd even closed the door. She crept out and went into her own room. She'd stay up here, just as she had planned. She'd brought along a Ruth Rendell novel that she'd found in the bookcase in her bedroom and which she couldn't wait to begin. She'd undress and lie in bed and read.

But first she'd have a cool shower. She went into the bathroom and began to pull off her dress. She was so hot, despite its thinness and its low-cut top. She'd already caught the sun, she saw. She'd soon tan in this weather. She'd have to make sure she applied plenty of suntan cream, though; she didn't want to turn an unbecoming crimson.

There was a knock on her door. She stuck her head through the doorway of the bathroom. 'Who is it?'

'Sebastian. What are you doing? I was expecting you downstairs.'

This was the last thing she'd expected. She'd thought once she was in her room, she'd be safe from any further pressure. Kathryn swiftly pulled the dress back on, zipping up the back once more, before opening the door and peering out.

'I was just about to climb into bed. I'm tired.'

'What rubbish!' he snorted. 'You slept for most of the afternoon. How can you be tired?'

A surge of annoyance swept through her at the shortness of his tone. And how did he know she'd slept this afternoon? Had he looked in on her? The thought of that disturbed her. You were at your most vulnerable at that moment. How dare he? Supposing she'd been snoring, as he'd once accused her of? Or worse, dribbling?

'We're going to have a bit of a party as it's our first night here. Maybe some dancing — ?' His narrowed gaze seared into her, burning her. At least, that was the way it felt.

Her pulses quickened at the mere thought of dancing with him, but she knew for the sake of her sanity, and not least her heart, that that was the last thing she should do. To be held in his arms, so close to him, would be akin to torture.

'No, really, I can't.'

His eyes darkened then, as his mouth tightened into a thin line. 'Not scared, are we?' he harshly demanded.

My God, he hadn't read her thoughts

again, had he? From somewhere, Lord knew where, she mustered up a short laugh. 'Whatever should I be scared of?' She even managed to sound scornful. Which considering the manner in which her emotions were see-sawing around, was something of an achievement.

'Me?'

'Don't be silly.' She tried very hard to sound as if she meant that. But as his next words proved, he wasn't fooled; not for a second.

'Of dancing with me, then?' His voice had deepened, become husky; seductively so. Blue eyes, their gaze suddenly intense, scorched her from beneath lowered lids. He knew darned well she was scared. Scared of what she might be tempted into. After all, he must have kissed her enough times now to suspect from her responses that she was strongly attracted to him. Still, she knew in that moment she'd have to do as he wanted. The wretched man was practically daring her. Challenging her. Was this his idea of fun? Tormenting the nanny? He was proving to be no better than Cassie. And what was Cassie going to say, seeing her future husband dancing with the nanny? And, come to that, what the hell was Sebastian thinking of, wanting to dance with her when the woman he loved was here, eager to be with him?

She put the thought, more or less, into words. 'It-It doesn't seem right.'

'What doesn't?'

'To dance with you. You are my employer, temporary or not.' She was tempted to add, 'And, more importantly, you're Cassie's lover.'

He stared at her in undisguised astonishment. 'I've never heard such rubbish.' His gaze hardened. 'I'm not leaving here until you agree.'

Defeated by his sheer determination, she sighed. 'Okay, okay. You win.' She'd have one dance and then leave the party. If she played her cards right, it didn't even have to be with him. There were two other men present after all, one completely unattached. The perfect partner.

She closed the door behind her and followed him down the stairs. Her heart was banging painfully against her ribcage. She dreaded to think what Cassie was going to say at the sight of Kathryn. She'd had enough of the other woman's catty remarks to last her a lifetime. She wouldn't care if she never saw her again. In fact, that would be eminently preferable.

But her hopes that with a spot of judicious management she could avoid dancing with Sebastian were swiftly dashed. As they walked out onto the terrace, he swung her and pulled her into his arms. Short of making an embarrassing scene, Kathryn could do nothing else but capitulate. Just as she'd anticipated, every one of her senses was catapulted into hyperdrive. Especially when he pulled her close to him and rested his cheek against her head.

If he did indeed know how she felt about him, then he was being needlessly cruel. And why would he want to torment Cassie? Was it all some sort of power game? A need to control things — people?

She took a steadying breath, fighting to ignore the feel of him so near; the feel of his arms tightening about her, pressing her even closer, ensuring that she felt every hard line of him. His breath fluttered the strands of her hair, caressing the skin of her face, making every nerve end tingle.

'There,' he murmured, his lips brushing her face as he spoke, 'that's not so bad, is it?'

And therein lay her problem. It wasn't bad, it was wonderful; totally right. It was as if she'd come home, back to where she belonged. They began to move to the slow rhythm of the music, their bodies perfectly attuned, as if they'd been born to dance together. Kathryn couldn't stop herself: she tilted her head back and stared up at him. His eyes met hers, their smouldering stare all but mesmerising her. Her breath caught in her throat; her lips parted. He did know how she felt. So, for the umpteenth time, she asked herself, what was his game? To make Cassie jealous? Why? There was no need. Cassie was only too eager to be with him. She sneaked a glance at the other woman. His plan — if that was what it was — was working. Cassie was staring at them, her expression one of pure vitriol. Kathryn pulled away from him, leaving a respectable gap between their bodies.

'Kathryn?'

'What?'

'I said — ' He looked and sounded amused now. ' — this isn't so bad, is it?'

'Oh, yes — um, I mean — no. It's okay.'

'Such enthusiasm,' he drily retorted, pulling her close once again.

Kathryn closed her eyes in despair. He must be able to detect her response to him. She was practically shuddering with longing. Tears stung her eyes, and suddenly she could stand the torment no longer. She tried to free herself.

'Kathryn?' He'd tightened his grip on her.

'I'm sorry, I can't do this — I have to

go.' And she tore herself free to all but run from him, desperate now to escape the danger, the danger of revealing exactly how she felt about him. He let her go, but she could feel his gaze upon her, the intensity of his stare tugging at her, trying to pull her back. She almost stopped and did as he so obviously wanted, but then she heard Cassie speak.

'Oh dear. What have you said to upset our little nanny?'

It was enough to propel her through the open French window, across the sitting room, into the hallway and up the stairs. By the time she got back to her room and closed the door behind her, the tears were flowing torrentially.

She threw herself onto the bed. How was she going to endure this? Had she just betrayed herself? Did he now know how much she loved him? Her face flamed. She covered it with her hands, asking herself how in God's name she could feel love for a man who had possibly driven his wife to her death.

Her sleep that night was punctuated

by dreams of Sebastian and Cassie together, making love. Come morning, however, a merciful calmness of sorts had returned to her. All she had to do to get through the remainder of this week, she told herself over and over, was to keep her distance from the man she loved. Shouldn't be too difficult.

* * *

And sure enough, it wasn't. For Sebastian seemed to have reached the same conclusion. Maybe he'd suffered from an unaccustomed bout of conscience and had sensed how uncomfortable he'd made her. Or maybe Cassie had shown her intense displeasure — jealousy even, and he'd decided it wasn't worth upsetting the woman he loved for mere moments of pleasure with another. His child's nanny, no less.

Lucy helped, taking Kathryn and Jamie out in their hired car most days, visiting nearby towns and beaches. She didn't know or care what Sebastian thought of this, and he didn't say anything. She and Lucy developed a close friendship. They turned out to be remarkably similar in their opinions and attitudes.

'You're good for Sebastian,' Lucy remarked at one point.

'How so?' Kathryn asked, slightly nervously.

'You don't treat him as some sort of god. It does him good to be talked back to now and again. Most of the people he knows just go along with whatever he says. It's a shame you have to leave,' Lucy went on, eyeing Kathryn as she did so. 'Jamie obviously loves you. Do you have to go?'

'I'm afraid so, yes.'

The evenings proved the most difficult times, although there was no more dancing. In fact, Cassie left after a few days to fly back to England on her own. Kathryn didn't know why. The thought did cross her mind that maybe she and Sebastian had had an argument of some sort. She certainly hadn't seemed very happy. Robert too had left, so only Lucy and Daniel remained. It made for a more peaceful and relaxed last couple of days, and an even deeper friendship developed between Kathryn and Lucy. They'd agreed to meet sometime in the not-too-distant future.

Even so, Kathryn was heartily relieved to be back in England. They arrived at Willow Court on the Sunday evening and Sebastian said, 'Take tomorrow off. Go and visit your parents.' Which Kathryn was glad to do.

Nothing had changed while she'd been away. Her mother was evasive about when she was having her investigation on her lump done — or maybe she simply didn't know. Her father still looked tired and harassed and was noticeably reluctant to talk about the trouble at work.

All in all, the day wasn't a particularly happy one.

14

Upon her return to Willow Court, Kathryn quietly let herself into the house and made for the stairs. As she did so, she heard voices coming from the library — men's voices. One, of course, was Sebastian's; the other she wasn't sure about. She thought it might be Jack. She'd only met him once, after all, and he hadn't got in touch as he'd promised. Sebastian's worries about her seeing him had been unfounded, after all. Yet she couldn't help wondering whether he'd been warned off by Sebastian.

She knew she was doing wrong, but she simply couldn't help herself. Lord! She was becoming a serial eavesdropper. That thought didn't deter her, however. Sebastian's voice literally drew her towards the closed door.

'The load that went missing on Thursday night was large enough to necessitate some form of transport. With no sign of a break-in, it must be someone inside — someone with legitimate access, either working alone or as part of a gang. One of the managers? I hate to think so, but it has to be. They're the only members of staff with keys. I don't want to come to this conclusion, but as the missing food is almost always from Kirkwood's department — well, you do the working out.'

Kathryn stiffened and moved closer to the library door, despite her every instinct shrieking 'Stop!' She didn't stop; she couldn't. She had to know what had happened. Her father hadn't mentioned a theft large enough to need transport when she'd asked him about it all. Thursday? That meant it had taken place while they were in France. Did someone ring Sebastian? And if so, why hadn't he said something to her? After all, it was her father who was under suspicion. Or had Sebastian not known till he returned to England?

Her unease intensified. Richard couldn't

be involved, surely? Yet as Sebastian had pointed out, he did have keys, and it was his department. She recalled Richard's troubled look when she'd quizzed him about it all. But still she refused to believe it; he was the most honest man she'd ever known. So why did a miniscule seed of doubt begin to plant its roots within her?

'Who's this Kirkwood then, that you're so unwilling to believe it's him?' the voice that could possibly be Jack's asked. 'I mean it was your decision not to notify the police until you got back.'

'I know, but it's Kathryn's father.'

'Oh God, yes — I'd forgotten her name is Kirkwood. That's damned awkward.'

So it was Jack. Kathryn stayed exactly where she was. She needed to hear whatever it was Sebastian was going to say.

'Quite. Even if he himself wasn't directly involved, he could have let whoever it was in, or passed the keys on.'

Kathryn froze. Richard had gone out on Thursday evening, he had told her that. But he'd said he'd met a friend for a drink. Truth or lie? Had he, in fact, used his keys to let someone inside? Participated, even? Or handed them over to someone else? No way. She'd never believe that of him; not in a million years.

She should warn him, though, that he was a suspect; chief suspect even, by the sound of things — shouldn't she? Even if, with all that he had to worry him at the moment, it was the last thing that he needed to hear.

She made a split-second decision. She wouldn't say anything; wouldn't pile more stress onto him. But she couldn't help asking herself why he hadn't he told her about this latest theft when she'd asked.

'I know you've put it off, and I quite understand why under the circumstances, but we have to call the police, Sebastian. It's been four days as it is. They're going to wonder why we've delayed. And you don't know that it was Kirkwood.'

Kathryn fled before she could hear Sebastian's reply to this. She didn't want to know what he intended to do. But more to the point, what should she do? Should she tell Sebastian that it couldn't possibly be her father? But if she did that, then she'd also have to confess to eavesdropping. And he must think in his own mind that Richard was the guilty party, or he'd have instructed the police to be called straight away. At least she could be grateful to him for that. Although she did wonder why he'd delayed; why anyone at Supreme Foods had delayed, come to that. Such uncertainty and indecision didn't match up with what she now knew about Sebastian.

She was no clearer in her mind as to what to do by the next morning, even though she'd lain awake going over and over all that had happened. She and Jamie ate breakfast together and then she handed him over to Joyce while she went to the library to find Sebastian and see what he wanted her to do for him.

He, too, looked as if he hadn't slept; his face was etched with lines of exhaustion, and even the tan he'd acquired in France seemed to have paled. 'Oh, there you are. I need to talk to you.'

Kathryn could tell by the expression on his face what it was he wished to talk about: her father and his possible involvement in the thefts of food from the factory. Her heart thundered but she said nothing. She couldn't — not without revealing the fact that she'd listened in to his conversation.

He paused as if to gather his thoughts. Then, without any preamble, he said, 'The thefts from Supreme Food . . . '

'Yes?' She tried desperately hard to sound as if she had no idea what he was about to say. She didn't know whether she succeeded or not.

'Quite a lot more went missing overnight on Thursday, enough to necessitate some method of transportation. There was no sign of a break-in, so whoever did it must have had keys.'

Still Kathryn didn't speak. Her breath stilled in her throat as she waited for him to go on, to put into words his belief that her father must somehow be involved in the theft.

'Which means the culprit must be someone who works for Supreme Foods, especially if you take into account the regular amounts that have been taken over the past weeks. As you probably know, the department in question is the one your father is in charge of and he, of course, has a key to the main building as well as his own department. I didn't want to do this but I really do have to notify the police now. It can't be allowed to go on, not thefts of this magnitude. They're bound to ask me who has access.'

'So what you're implying by telling me first — warning me, in other words — is that my father is a suspect?'

He nodded. 'I'm sorry, Kathryn, but it seems the only explanation. The thief must have had keys on this occasion.

The police will undoubtedly reach the same conclusion.'

'Wouldn't that be rather stupid of him, being the manager — and as such, the only person in that department with the means of entry? I mean, under the circumstances, he must know he'd be the first one to come under suspicion. And why hasn't someone notified the police before this if it happened on Thursday? Won't that look suspicious in itself? Did you know it had happened?'

He nodded. 'Jack phoned me on Friday morning while we were in France. I told him to hang fire until I returned.'

'But why didn't he simply ring the police when he discovered what had happened? Why ring you?'

'Because we hadn't wanted to get the police involved, and I'd told him to check with me first. It's always better if one can sort this kind of theft out internally. And it hadn't been large amounts anyway to begin with, not like this time. The police probably wouldn't have been interested.'

'Is it because of me,' she blurted, 'that you haven't informed the police? Because I'm his daughter?'

He nodded again.

'I know it can't be my father,' she cried. 'He'd never do such a thing. There must be some other explanation. Let me talk to him first, at least warn him that you're calling the police in, please. I'll go this evening.'

Sebastian regarded her doubtfully. 'Well . . . '

'Please — there are circumstances that you know nothing about.' Tears sprang to her eyes at the notion of what this would do to her father. But it wasn't only that. What was really bothering her was the suspicion that the anxiety he'd been going through over her mother had somehow provoked him into such uncharacteristic behaviour. Sent him over the edge, in other words. She prayed that he had a solid alibi for Thursday night, because if he didn't . . . But no, that wouldn't do, because as Sebastian had said the evening before, he could easily have passed his keys on to someone else; at least, that was what the police would think. And then, overriding of all of this was the question of what it would do to her mother's fragile state of mind. The tears brimmed faster and became unstoppable, spilling over to cascade down her face. This, on top of everything else — it was too much. 'S-sorry.' Furious with herself for this display of weakness, she dashed them away.

'Kathryn — ' Sebastian took a step towards her. ' — this is the last thing I wanted.'

'A-and me,' she sobbed helplessly.

'Of course I'll give you time to talk to your father. We've waited this long; another day or so won't matter.' He reached her and putting his arms around her, pulled her close, comfortingly close. And she was sure that that was all he intended to begin with, to simply offer her some comfort, some measure of reassurance. But the second she was in his arms, as it always did, everything changed. A flame ignited between them and instantly he was kissing her hungrily, passionately.

Kathryn couldn't help herself. Just like the other times it happened, her resistance melted at his touch and she clung to him, desperately responding with everything that was in her. Nothing else mattered in that moment; nothing.

And if nothing else mattered to her, apparently it didn't inhibit Sebastian either. He enfolded her completely within the circle of his arms. It was as if they became one. He deepened the kiss, catapulting Kathryn's senses into a frenzy. She heard someone moan and realised it was her. What was she doing? Again? What was wrong with her? That she couldn't seem to resist him? That she kept letting him do this? She should be thinking of her father's predicament, not her own desires, longings. And he belonged to Cassie; she knew that, had proof of it in that letter she'd found. She jerked her head away from his and stared up at him, her eyes wide and shadowed with uncertainty. He looked back from beneath heavy lids. Passion smouldered at her, scorching her. Using both hands, she shoved him away from her.

'Kathryn?' His voice was throaty as he reached for her once again.

'No — don't. How could you?' she blurted, deftly evading his grasp. 'This isn't the time.' She almost went on, 'Especially if you're on the verge of marrying another woman.' She didn't. Because to admit knowing that meant she'd also have to reveal that she'd found the incriminating letter and had said nothing to anyone. Although that could then force him to admit that he loved Cassie.

'It never is,' he muttered. 'But you're right. I apologise. It's entirely inappropriate.'

'It was, so maybe you'd like to tell me what you want me to do today.'

* * *

Yet even taking into account the strain she was under with regards to her father's situation, as well as her own desperately confused state of mind, her day, in the end, proved an astonishingly productive one. She'd managed to put all thoughts of what she had to do later to the back of her mind and concentrated wholly upon her work. This consisted of typing a stack of Sebastian's correspondence and adding entries to bring his diary right up to date, as well as dealing with several phone calls. By three o'clock everything was finished and she left the office that he'd told her to use and went to find Jamie.

The little boy hurled himself joyfully at her. 'Where have you been, Kathryn?' he demanded to know.

Kathryn hugged him. 'I've been helping your daddy, but I'm all yours now.'

It wasn't until seven o'clock that she managed to leave the house. She'd seen nothing more of Sebastian since their encounter that morning. She just hoped he'd done what he said he'd do and delayed telling the police. She drove swiftly to her parents' house and let herself in.

'Mum, Dad,' she called. 'It's me, Kathryn.'

'What are you doing here? It's not Sunday.'

It was Jess, coming down the stairs. She was smiling and wearing the earrings that Kathryn had admired before.

'Where are you off to?' Kathryn asked.

'To meet Fitz.'

'Jess, are you sure about him? I mean . . . '

'What? What do you mean?' Every trace of good humour fled, to be replaced by angry indignation. Kathryn nibbled at her lip, annoyed at her conspicuous lack of tact. Jess continued: 'That he doesn't come up to your rigorously high standards; that he doesn't conform to the dull, boring style that you go for? Is that what you're trying to say in your oh-so-subtle way? Because if you are then just come out with it.'

'That's not what I meant.'

'Didn't you? Funny, because that's exactly what it sounded like. Oh, and I take it you didn't speak to your boss about my job?'

'I did, but it did no good.'

'Well, thanks for nothing.'

'Jess, I tried; I really did.'

'Yeah, right. If it's the parents you want, they're in the garden.' Jess swept from the house, banging the door behind her in a final angry gesture of defiance.

15

Sighing in the knowledge that she'd once more upset her sister — although in truth it was becoming increasingly difficult not to, as relations between them had deteriorated to such an extent — Kathryn walked into the kitchen, the only route to the garden at the back of the house, and let herself out. She should have known better than to say anything to Jess. All she'd achieved was to make her even more determined to go on seeing Fitz. She should learn to mind her own business. She would from now on.

She saw her parents at once. They were sitting beneath a rose-smothered pergola that her father had constructed a couple of years before, glasses of wine in their hands. They were smiling and talking, for once happy and untroubled. She wondered if her mother had received good news. But surely, she'd have rung Kathryn?

'Hi, Mum, Dad.' She beamed at them as she walked towards them.

'Kathryn, darling, what on earth are you doing here?' her mother gasped. 'Not that it's not lovely to see you.'

Kathryn bent and kissed her father and then did the same with her mother. 'Have you heard any more about when you'll get those tests done? It's dragging on a bit.'

A shadow crossed Helen's face with the question and Kathryn suddenly knew without a shadow of doubt that the display of smiling happiness was solely for Richard's benefit. Beneath that veneer, she was still a deeply troubled woman. It was all there in her eyes — the pain, the anguish, dimming the brightness of her smile. 'I went last week.'

'You didn't say.'

'I couldn't. You were in France.'

'I was here yesterday.'

'I know, but I didn't want to say

anything until I had the results. And that could take a week or two, apparently.'

'Okay. Well, ring me the instant you get them, won't you? Dad — ' She glanced at her father then. ' — can we have a word?'

'Yes, of course. What is it?'

Kathryn hesitated. She didn't want to discuss the matter of Richard's possible implication in Thursday's robbery in front of her mother, as it would only give her something else to worry about. But if she asked to see her father alone, Helen would want to know why. 'Um — it's nothing much.' Inspiration struck. 'There's something wrong with the car. Can you have a look before I take it to a garage and maybe have a huge bill?'

'Of course I will.' He looked pleased. He'd always fancied himself as a bit of a mechanic; sadly, he wasn't. His well-intentioned but unskilled attempts to put things right invariably resulted in a far greater problem than the original had been. He glanced enquiringly at his wife.

'You go, darling,' Helen urged. 'I'll stay here and enjoy the evening sunshine and my wine.' She leant back into her chair, closing her eyes as she did so.

Richard followed Kathryn inside, through the kitchen and into the hallway. She stopped there. Richard looked at her nervously. He must have read something on her face because he instantly asked, 'What is it? What's wrong? Is it Jess?' His kindly face twisted into an expression of fatherly concern. 'I know she's terribly upset about losing her job.'

'No, Dad, it's you.' The words came out far more abruptly than she'd intended. She gnawed at her bottom lip. It wasn't like her to be so . . . well, brutal, she supposed.

'Me?' His expression darkened.

'I've been talking to Sebastian. Actually, to be strictly accurate, he's been talking to me.'

'Ye-es?' From Richard's look of apprehension, she guessed he knew what was coming.

'It's about the thefts at Supreme Foods. Did you know a large load was taken on Thursday night?'

'Of course I knew. I work there.'

'Then why didn't you say something when I was here yesterday?'

'I didn't want to worry you about my business affairs, and — well, I didn't want to say anything in front of your mother; she doesn't know it happened. She thinks the thefts have all stopped. She does worry so, and I-I didn't want to add to the strain that she's under at the moment,' he finished lamely in the face of Kathryn's exasperation.

'He's calling in the police.'

'Aah.'

'And you'll be chief suspect, as a key-holder and manager of that particular department.'

At that, Richard's head jerked up. He stared at her, looking frightened suddenly. 'Did he tell you that?'

Kathryn nodded.

'I suppose I should have expected it. It would have been a simple matter to let myself in — or someone else. I was hoping that my long and loyal record with the company would stand for something. Clearly not.' His shoulders slumped and he sounded wearily resigned; defeated, even.

'And you were out Thursday evening, weren't you?'

'I was.' His shoulders slumped even further and Kathryn wouldn't have believed that possible.

'Dad — I have to ask you this. It wasn't you, was it? I would understand if it was. You've been under a great deal of strain lately.'

'Kathryn — ' Richard's face blanched until it was the colour of putty. ' — I would never — never, do you hear me? — do anything like that. Never. Surely you know that?'

'I'm sorry, Dad, but I had to ask.'

'Of course, but — you do believe me, don't you?' He looked so careworn, so old all of a sudden, that Kathryn's heart almost broke in two.

'Yes . . . yes. I never really had any doubt about you. I told Sebastian so.'

'Thank you, darling. Kathryn?'

'Yes?'

'Please don't mention this to your mother. I don't know how she'd react at the moment. It could prove too much; the last straw.'

'I know, and I won't. I only came to warn you that the police will be coming to Supreme Foods to interview you — amongst others, I'm sure. But — ' She stared at her father, the doubts beginning to surface about what they were doing — hiding. ' — although I also decided not to say anything in front of Mum, it's bound to come out eventually that you're a suspect. Mum will have to know then.'

'Yes, but later rather than sooner, hopefully. If we can get all this business of the test results behind us first. I can't tell her now; she's got enough on her plate as it is.'

But Kathryn wasn't sure he'd be allowed the time for that.

* * *

As far as Kathryn knew, the police duly turned up at Supreme Foods and started their investigation. Her father didn't ring, so he couldn't have been arrested; and her mother would certainly have been on the phone straight away if that had been the case. There also was no news about her mother's test results. On the whole, though, the lack of urgency over it all was reassuring. The doctors must be fairly confident it wasn't cancer, surely? Still, Kathryn increasingly felt as if she were existing in some sort of weird limbo.

* * *

And then, as if all this wasn't bad enough, the completely unexpected happened.

Matt returned from Dubai.

It was Rosie who rang and told her. 'I've just seen him. He didn't spot me, so I thought the best thing I could do was ring you and warn you.'

'Thanks, Rosie.'

She ended the call, her expression reflective. Why was Matt back? He'd had a much longer contract this time. Oh well, it was nothing to do with her. Not any longer.

She'd put Jamie to bed and had returned to her room prior to joining Joyce for supper when she heard the doorbell ring. The business of dining with Sebastian no longer happened. More often than not, he wasn't even home by then. She had no idea where he went — to Cassie's probably. She firmly dismissed the disturbing images that that thought induced.

She listened, wondering who would be calling at this time. She heard the indistinguishable murmur of voices, of which one was Joyce's, and then the housekeeper was calling, 'Kathryn, it's someone for you.'

With no sense of what was about to happen, Kathryn lightly ran down the stairs. 'I've put him in the sitting room,' Joyce told her before hurrying back to the kitchen.

Him? Oh no. Matt wouldn't come here, would he? But who else could it be? Her father? Unlikely. With a growing disquiet, Kathryn walked into the room.

Her suspicions were confirmed. Matt stood there.

'Matt? What are you doing here?' She wasn't pleased and didn't bother to disguise that.

'Didn't you think I'd want to see you?' he calmly said. 'Presumably you knew I was back?'

'Yes, Rosie mentioned it. She spotted you. But it didn't occur to me you'd come here. I was under the impression things were over between us.'

She stopped talking. Matt's face had turned a deep puce and he was rubbing at the back of his neck, a sure sign that he was disturbed about something.

'That's what I wanted to talk to you about,' he muttered.

Kathryn silently waited for him to go on.

'I'm so sorry. Can you ever forgive me?' He looked uncharacteristically anguished.

'Is that why you've come? To ask my forgiveness? He nodded. 'I forgave you long ago, Matt. I've had too much else to occupy me to spend time moping over what might have been.' She spoke briskly; harshly.

Matt, visibly shocked by this, muttered, 'B-but — '

'So.' Kathryn suspected that that wasn't his sole reason for coming here. 'Why did you want to see me, really? If it's to invite me to your wedding, well, I'm sorry but I'll be far too busy to attend.'

'There isn't going to be a wedding,' he blurted.

It was now Kathryn's turn to be shocked. 'What?'

'We're over — Janice and me.'

'B-but what about the baby?'

'She lost it and without that, she didn't want me.'

'I'm sorry.'

'I'm not. We weren't really that well suited.'

Kathryn studied him then, her head cocked to one side. 'So if I've got this right, she's dumped you and you've come running back to me. Good ol' Kathryn, the last resort so to speak.'

'No, it's not like that at all.'

'What is it like?'

'I still love you. I never really stopped. I made a terrible mistake ending things between us.'

She gave a snort of contemptuous laughter. 'Really? You could have fooled me.'

He eyed her. 'You never used to be this . . . hard.'

'No? Well, maybe I have you to thank for that change of character. I'm not so easily duped anymore.'

'Don't, please don't. I love you.'

'Matt, you cheated on me. Why

would I trust you now? And I don't think a relationship with someone who's half a world away would be any more successful than before.'

'I'd come back.'

She frowned. 'I thought you had a contract to stay?'

'I do, but it could be broken.'

Kathryn stared at him. How could she ever have believed he was the man for her? 'Well that says it all really. You've got no sense of loyalty, no staying power. And to think I wasted two years of my life waiting for you.' She turned away, making ready to leave the room; leave him. She yanked the door open. 'I'd like you to go now.'

'Kathryn, wait.'

She whirled and walked back to him. 'No. I will never wait for you again. Now, please go.' And this time she pointed at the open door.

'No, I won't, and I'm not accepting what you're saying. I know you don't mean it.' Grimly, he strode to her and grabbed her by the shoulders. He yanked her into him and held her tightly against him, so tightly it was painful.

'Matt, don't do this.'

'Don't do what?' he taunted. 'This?' He lowered his head and kissed her. She thought she smelled whiskey. 'You used to like it — my God, you loved it,' he muttered against her lips. 'Couldn't get enough of it.'

'No.' She began to struggle, fruitlessly. He was far too strong for her; he was also drunk, she realised. His hold on her tightened and his kiss roughened. He dragged her to the nearby settee and forced her down backwards onto it. Kathryn felt the beginnings of fear. She struggled even harder. 'Matt, please,' she groaned.

He dropped down onto her, effectively imprisoning her beneath him. His mouth covered hers again, brutally this time.

'What the hell's going on here?' an icy voice demanded to know.

It was Sebastian.

Kathryn closed her eyes in horrified mortification. Matt leapt to his feet, leaving her lying there, mouth bruised, clothes awry, shaking with the shock of what had just happened. Despite this, she managed to sit up, not daring to look at Sebastian. When she did, his eyes were the bleakest and coldest she'd ever seen. His face was a granite mask.

'Would you like to explain, Kathryn — ' His voice was low and menacing. ' — just what was going on then, in my house?'

Quickly she stood up, even though every inch of her was shaking, quivering. Sebastian's gaze raked her; it was as if he were looking at the lowliest of mortals.

'Uh — th-this is Matt. You met him.'

'I remember — in the Red Lion.' He swept his icy gaze to Matt now. 'I thought you were in Dubai.' His tone was one of utter contempt.

'I-I was. I've come back for Kathryn,' Matt stammered.

'Oh really?' If she'd thought Sebastian's

expression a fearsome one before, now it positively terrified her. He looked capable of anything. 'And is Kathryn going with you?'

'No.' Kathryn interrupted before Matt could utter any more damning words. 'I'm not and I'd like you to leave now, Matt.'

'No,' Matt shouted, 'I won't.'

With that, Sebastian's one eyebrow lifted so high it all but disappeared into his hairline. 'Oh yes you will,' he ground out. 'You either go voluntarily or I throw you out. Take your pick.'

But Matt knew when he was beaten. He held up both hands in surrender. 'Okay, okay. There's no need for that.' He glanced at Kathryn. 'Does this mean we're over?'

'I think you can safely assume that's precisely what she means,' Sebastian calmly put in. His anger had vanished and he was once again the cool, self-possessed individual that Kathryn was so familiar with.

Even so, Kathryn wished the ground

would open up and swallow her, because Sebastian had now turned his attention back to her and she didn't care for his expression at all. It signified that the hour of retribution was near. And she dreaded to think what that might be. The sack, for sure — finally. Her heart ached at the mere notion of leaving the small boy she'd come to love so dearly.

Without another word, Matt left the room, and seconds later Kathryn heard the front door close behind him. For a split second, she almost called him back. She didn't really want to be alone with Sebastian.

Within an instant, she knew she'd been right to be afraid. 'So,' Sebastian drawled, 'tell me. How many men do you want, Kathryn?'

'Wh-what?' she stammered.

'Well, first there was Matt, then there was Jack, now Matt — again. Who else do you have waiting on the sidelines? I really would like some sort of warning of who's going to show up in my house.' And he sarcastically stressed the 'my'.

'Firstly, I don't want any . . . men.' She took her cue from him and sarcastically emphasized the single word. 'And if you want the truth, even if I do, it's none of your business.'

'Oh, but it is. As I've just said, this is my house, my home, and my son is here — upstairs. What if he'd come in on the little scene that I've just witnessed?' He sneered at her, his top lip curling as he did so.

Kathryn felt something shrivel inside of her. He despised her. 'I'm sorry, but I didn't invite him here.'

'No? You went along with him though, didn't you?'

'No!' she cried. 'I didn't.'

'Well, you could have fooled me. You were groaning, murmuring his name.' His mouth twisted with distaste.

'No, that wasn't how it was.'

'Really? Well, if it's lovemaking that you want, I'm here,' and to Kathryn's horror, he took a step towards her, and just as Matt had done, dragged her into him. She winced in pain but that was swiftly forgotten as he captured her swollen lips. His kiss was every bit as rough as Matt's had been, his arms just as tight around her. Yet, to Kathryn's horror, and as she invariably did, she returned his kiss — right before he pushed her away. 'Now get out of my sight,' he ordered, and swung away from her as if he truly meant it and couldn't bear to look at her any longer.

Kathryn ran from the room, suppressing her sobs of anguish and humiliation by pressing her hands against her mouth. She held her cries in until she reached her room, whereupon she threw herself onto the bed and let all her heartache out.

16

Despite what had happened between herself and Sebastian, Kathryn couldn't bring herself to leave Willow Court and, astonishingly, he hadn't asked her to. Although that could be because she hadn't seen anything of him.

She and Jamie were growing ever closer, and that worried her deeply. How would he cope when it was time for her to leave? How would she cope, come to that? She'd grown to love the small boy — just as she had his father — in the short time she'd been at Willow Court. Yet apparently Sebastian still hadn't found anyone to replace her. Was he even looking?

Kathryn was split between a feeling of relief and one of dread: relief that she didn't have to leave yet, and dread that if she stayed for very much longer, her heart would surely break when that day arrived — as surely it would eventually. Because she simply couldn't imagine never again feeling Jamie's arms around her neck as he kissed her good night, or not hearing his mischievous chuckle when she did something stupid. But over and above all of that was the unwelcome notion of some other woman having the care of him. Cassie, for instance.

* * *

And then, one afternoon, Sebastian strode into the room where Kathryn was working. Startled, she looked up at him. He'd been leaving her a written list of the tasks he wanted her to do, so not surprisingly she'd found herself deciding that he was actively avoiding her. She could understand that. He probably couldn't bear to look at her after what he'd assumed had been happening between her and Matt.

However, there wasn't any sign of the rage he'd exhibited then as he told her without any sort of preamble, 'Your father's handed in his notice with immediate effect. Did you know he was going to do that?'

'No.' Kathryn was horrified, and it drove everything else from her mind — chiefly, how she should behave with him after their last stormy encounter. Richard must be in a truly desperate state of mind to resign. He loved his job; it had been his life. He'd worked there for over twenty-five years, industriously making his way up to the managerial position that he held today. He couldn't — mustn't throw all that away.

'Go and see him now,' Sebastian commanded. 'Tell him to withdraw it at once. His resignation just makes him look guilty — the police sound all set to arrest him.'

* * *

Sebastian's tone was one of such urgency that Kathryn didn't need a second bidding. She ran from the house, climbed into her car, and headed for home. Despite what she'd overheard him saying to Jack, he must believe her father innocent, or he wouldn't have said what he just had. She strode into the house when she got there, calling, 'Dad, where are you?'

Helen poked her head around the kitchen door, from where were coming delicious smells of cooking meat. 'He's not here yet, darling.'

But even as she spoke the words, the front door opened and Richard walked in. His face was as grey as the jacket he was wearing; his eyes were blank holes, his mouth a grim line.

'Richard,' Helen gasped. 'What on earth's wrong? You look ghastly. Has something happened?'

'You could say that. I've resigned,' he told them. 'As from now.'

'B-but why?' Helen stuttered.

'I'm sick of living beneath the burden of suspicion. Everyone thinks I'm the guilty party — the police investigation has seen to that.'

Helen's face was now as ashen as her husband's. 'What? I thought the thefts had all stopped.'

'Dad — ' Kathryn went to him. ' — Sebastian told me what you'd done. That's why I'm here. He also said that you must withdraw your resignation immediately. Such an action will only confirm your guilt in the police's eyes. He thinks they're about to arrest you.'

'Richard,' Helen wailed, 'why didn't you tell me? I'm your wife, for heaven's sake — you're supposed to talk to me, tell me things.'

Neither Kathryn nor Richard answered her.

'I'm positive Sebastian doesn't believe you're guilty,' Kathryn said. 'If you ring him now . . . '

But it was too late. There was a loud rap on the door and a man's voice called, 'Open the door, please, Mr Kirkwood. It's the police.'

What happened next was like a living nightmare to Kathryn and Helen. All

Kathryn could think was they should have told her, warned her. Because Helen looked to be on the verge of complete collapse. This didn't seem to matter to the two policemen who entered the house, however, once Kathryn opened the door to them. They took Richard away with them, for further questioning, they said, and Kathryn and Helen were left, stunned and disbelieving.

'C-can they do that?' Helen asked, looking for all the world like a bewildered child. 'To an innocent man?'

'Sadly, yes. These days, I'm afraid, their philosophy seems to be that you're guilty till proved innocent,' Kathryn bitingly retorted. 'I'm ringing Sebastian. He's the only one who can sort this out — I hope,' she muttered under her breath. All she could think was, what would his arrest do to Richard's state of mind, already dramatically impaired by the worry surrounding his wife's health?

Within minutes of her phone call, Sebastian was at the door. Kathryn let him in. Helen was too distraught to do anything other than weep, 'This can't be happening — it can't be. Richard would never steal from anyone.'

Sebastian took Kathryn to one side and murmured, 'I've rung my own solicitor. He's on his way to the police station as I speak. He'll have your father out of there so quick . . . '

Now it was Kathryn's turn to wail, 'How could this be happening? My father would never — someone else must have got hold of his keys; it's the only explanation.'

'I agree. The question is, who? He said he sometimes lets members of the staff have them because they're on the key ring that holds all the other keys to store cupboards and such-like. But he assured me they're all absolutely trustworthy and have been with the firm for years. And they couldn't have kept the keys anyway; your father would have known. It doesn't make sense — none of it does.'

Helen had begun to weep even harder now.

'Mrs Kirkwood, this will be sorted out, I promise you that.' Sebastian went to her and laid a comforting hand upon her shoulder. 'You have my word,' he gently went on. He then passed her a snowy white handkerchief.

'Oh thank you, thank you.' She gazed up at him through tear-drenched eyes. 'You're being so kind, so helpful.'

Just as Sebastian had promised, Richard was released within the hour, whereupon he returned home to where his wife, daughter and employer were waiting for him.

'Thank you, Grant,' Richard said, at the same time energetically shaking his employer's hand. 'If you hadn't sent your solicitor along, I'd still be there, probably under arrest and sitting in a cell.'

'Do they believe you're innocent though, Richard?' Helen tearfully asked.

'I don't know. The police don't give much away, unfortunately. They've let me go for the moment; that's the main thing.'

* * *

It was just a few minutes short of eight thirty by the time Sebastian and Kathryn left to return to Willow Court. Richard had promised to return to work the following day. So for the moment at least, all seemed well.

They pulled their cars onto the forecourt, one behind the other. Sebastian led the way into the house, to be greeted by Jamie's cries from above.

'Daddy, Kathryn, where have you been?'

Sebastian and Kathryn looked at each other and both headed for the little boy's room. He was sitting up in bed, rubbing at his eyes and crying noisily. Joyce was already there, trying to comfort him. 'Here they are, my duck. He didn't want me,' she chuckled, 'so if you don't mind, I'll leave you to it.'

'Thank you, Joyce, for putting him to bed.' Sebastian smiled at his housekeeper as she left the room. 'Now, my lad.' He swung back to his son. 'What's all this about? You should be fast asleep. Do you know what time it is?'

'No. Where have you been, Daddy?' He sounded indignant now, rather than distressed. 'And Kathryn, I needed you. I woke up and you weren't here.'

'Oh darling, I'm sorry.' She went and perched on the edge of his bed. 'But my daddy needed me.'

'You didn't read to me and didn't say goodbye. Joyce tried,' he told her, 'but she doesn't do it right.'

He was pouting at her. She hugged him to her, her heart swelling with love as she kissed the top of his head.

'Never mind,' she said, 'I'll make up for that tomorrow evening. I promise.'

He nestled his head into her shoulder, his eyes shining as he asked, loudly enough for his father to hear, 'Will you be my mummy, Kathryn? Tell her, Daddy — tell her she has to be my mummy.' All traces of his tears gone now, he swept his gaze back to Kathryn. 'You'd like to marry my daddy, wouldn't you?'

For once, Kathryn was at a complete loss as to how to reply. Jamie, as if sensing this, grinned at his father.

'Go on, Daddy, ask her.'

Sebastian, too, looked at a loss as to how to respond. However, his recovery seemed to be faster than Kathryn's, who was still wildly casting around for a diplomatic and appropriate refusal. He strode across to his son from the doorway where he'd been standing and said, 'Right, that's enough. Time for sleep.'

'But you haven't asked her, Daddy.'

'Time enough for that tomorrow.' He glanced at Kathryn as if to say 'humour him for now' before gently easing the small boy from Kathryn's embrace. 'It's late.'

'Read me a story, Daddy.' Jamie obviously wasn't going to give up easily. 'You sit here.' He patted the other side of the bed to the one upon which Kathryn had been sitting. Kathryn started to get up, planning to leave father and son alone together, but Jamie stopped her by the simple expedient of grabbing hold of her hand and instructing, in a tone that wouldn't be denied, 'No, you stay there, Kathryn.'

For a four-year-old, he was demonstrating an extraordinary ability to manipulate the situation for his own ends. Kathryn could do nothing else but stay. And so there they were, seemingly a family, as Sebastian read a story from Jamie's favourite book.

* * *

The following morning while she and Jamie were in the kitchen eating their breakfast, Sebastian strode in and, to her astonishment, asked, 'Who fancies a trip to the country? I'm sure Joyce would fix us a picnic. The Cotswolds would be good. The sun is shining, and a nice day is promised.' He looked at Kathryn, his eyes questioning; quizzical.

Jamie didn't hesitate. He instantly clapped his hands, shrieking, 'Yes, yes, a day out!'

Kathryn refrained from any such

display of exuberance, her first consideration being the fact that she had quite a lot of office work to do. Her hours spent working as Sebastian's PA had increased until she now did some each day just to keep on top of it. The second consideration was how she and Sebastian would manage to spend a whole day together in the wake of that disturbing episode with Matt and what had followed. She began to make excuses. 'Well,' she began, 'I do have all that data to enter for you.'

But Sebastian calmly waved her protest aside. 'After the troubles and traumas of yesterday, I think we deserve a little holiday. The work will still be there tomorrow.' It was as if nothing had ever happened between them. Had he decided to put it all behind him and forget what had happened? It was certainly looking that way.

Jamie now began to wave his arms around. His enthusiasm knew no bounds. Kathryn and Sebastian soon heard why. 'Yes, yes. We'll be a proper family.'

Where was all this coming from? Kathryn wondered bemusedly. Was it solely the result of not having a mother in his life? Compassion for the little boy engulfed her. The least she could do was to spend the day with him and his father. It could possibly be the last opportunity she'd have, because she knew she'd soon have to leave — for her own salvation if nothing else.

'Okay,' she agreed, slightly nervously, 'you've convinced me. A day out would be nice.'

* * *

So that was what they did. Joyce packed what looked like enough food for a dozen people, at least, and they — along with the hamper — piled into a brand-new and extremely luxurious Range Rover; there was no sign of the Mercedes today. Jamie chattered non-stop as Kathryn clipped him into his safety seat in the rear. She climbed in alongside him and buckled her own seat belt.

Sebastian swivelled his head and demanded, 'What are you doing?'

'Fastening my seat belt.'

'No, I meant why are you sitting back there? Come and sit in the front. Good Lord, do you want me to feel like a chauffeur?'

'Um — well, um . . . ' Kathryn started to protest. It didn't seem fitting, somehow. She was, after all, just the nanny, albeit the temporary nanny.

His gaze met hers via the interior mirror. For once, he appeared almost nervous. However, his confident words swiftly undermined that impression. 'I won't bite. Promise.' In fact, he sounded as if he were teasing her.

Kathryn, taking his assurance at face value and not wanting to embark upon an argument in front of Jamie, meekly did as she was told. It was as she buckled herself into the front seat belt that Jamie smugly told her, 'Mummies always sit in the front, next to the daddies.'

Kathryn decided to ignore that, although she did wonder if he'd been taking lessons from his father in self-assurance. She also ignored the slight tugging of amusement at the corner of Sebastian's mouth. Although it did lead her to wonder if they were ganging up on her; and if they were, at whose bidding?

An hour or so later they were in the heart of the beautiful Cotswold Hills. Their first stop was for coffee in the picture postcard town of Broadway, and once they'd satisfied their thirst they strolled along the main street, window shopping. They passed a place which was selling all sorts of fancy goods. Kathryn had a weakness for this sort of shop, so she stopped to admire the display of jewellery in the window. Some pieces were clearly antique and very expensive, but it was one particular pair of earrings that caught her eye. They were almost identical to the ones that Jess had been wearing; in fact, they were identical. Kathryn stared at the price ticket attached to them in astonishment.

One hundred and twenty-five pounds.

17

Kathryn's feeling of disquiet over how Fitz would have had the wherewithal to pay that much for a pair of earrings eventually passed. She shouldn't be so quick to judge, just because he looked . . . well, different. Jess was clearly fond of him. She'd take her cue from her sister and trust in his honesty; his integrity.

They returned to the car and went off in search of a suitable place to stop and eat their picnic lunch. It didn't take them long to find somewhere secluded and shielded from the road by a high hedgerow. The three of them left the vehicle to negotiate a somewhat uneven stretch of daisy-speckled grass to settle themselves beneath the branches of a massive horse chestnut tree.

Kathryn began to unpack the hamper, discovering smoked salmon and cream cheese sandwiches, miniature quiches, bowls of dressed salad leaves, crispy bread, more cheese and a selection of fruit. There was also a bottle of wine and two glasses. For Jamie, Joyce had included a bottle of mineral water, with some cheese and pickle sandwiches — his favourite.

'My goodness!' she exclaimed. 'Joyce has done us proud. It's a positive feast.'

All the time she'd been unpacking the food and spreading it on the tablecloth that Joyce had also thoughtfully provided, she'd been achingly aware of Sebastian's gaze following her every move. He'd sat down and then stretched out his long legs, crossing them at the ankles before leaning back to prop himself on one elbow as he lazily unscrewed the cap on the bottle of wine. Jamie, overflowing with the inexhaustible energy that was so typical of a four-year-old, had run off straight away, leaving them alone as he raced around on the grass, stopping every now and again to pick from the profusion of wild flowers that grew all around them.

Eventually, driven by the need to alleviate the heightening tension between herself and Sebastian with no Jamie to ease things along with his chatter, Kathryn said, 'I've been meaning to thank you.'

'Whatever for?' Sebastian's gaze now narrowed at her.

'For the way in which you helped my father. For believing in his innocence. Many people wouldn't have — didn't, in fact. That was the main reason for him resigning. He couldn't stand the suspicion from his workmates any longer; they all thought he'd done it. He is the holder of the keys, after all.'

She turned away from his penetrating gaze and concentrated on placing the food onto the various plates that Joyce had also provided, ostensibly engrossed in arranging things attractively, appetisingly. Still, no mention had been made of Matt or the scene that had ensued. It left her with a feeling of strain in Sebastian's presence. In fact, she was beginning to wish he would mention it; she could then defend herself and tell him that Matt had forced himself on her. As it was, she was reluctant to be the one to raise the subject.

After a moment or two, Sebastian slowly said, 'I couldn't see how anyone capable of stealing from his place of work could possibly have someone like you for a daughter.'

The words were quietly said, but they were unmistakably sincere. Could he have guessed what had happened that day with Matt? He'd certainly got over his rage with her, so maybe he had.

She turned her head to look at him again, but heavy lids had lowered, shielding his thoughts from her. It was something he was particularly adept at and it maddened her each and every time he did it.

A blush of gratification fanned her cheeks as she said, 'Well, thank you for that.'

'No, I want to thank you,' he went on, 'for helping me out like you are — and for not leaving us after-after — '

She sensed what he was trying to say.

'After the way I behaved.' It strengthened her certainty that, once he'd calmed down, he'd guessed what had really happened. A huge feeling of relief filled her.

'Daddy, Kathryn, look — look what I've found.' It was Jamie, and he was holding something out for them to see. It was a ladybird. 'Look, Kathryn. See — a ladybird.'

'Yes, darling, but be careful you don't squash it.' She spoke absently, her gaze riveted once more upon Sebastian. He wasn't looking at her, however; he was staring into the far distance, his expression one of bleakness and brooding.

'No, I won't. Look — I'll let it fly away.' He flung the tiny insect up into the air, watching gleefully as it took wing and swiftly disappeared. He ran after it, chuckling with delight.

Kathryn decided to go for it. She'd never get a better opportunity; here they were away from the house, alone. She would ask Sebastian about Sara and why he thought she'd done what she had, as well as about Cassie's role in his life — something she desperately wanted to know. 'Um — there's something I want to ask you; something I don't understand.' She paused. Did she have the courage to do this? Would it end in yet another bitter row? Taking a deep breath, she went for it. 'Why would Sara choose to end her life in such a terrible way?'

Sebastian looked surprised at first, but once that had subsided, thoughtful. Without speaking he poured them both a glass of wine and then said, 'She hadn't been happy for quite a while.' He handed Kathryn her glass and then reclined back, once again staring into the far distance, leaving Kathryn feeling excluded; shut out. But then he began to speak again. 'We shouldn't have married in the first place. We weren't right for each other. She quickly knew that, as I did. I hadn't realised just how unhappy she was, though, and I should have. Maybe then I could have prevented . . .'

His expression darkened as he lapsed into a brooding silence once more, and she knew he wasn't going to say anything else; certainly not mention his affair with Cassie. She could, she supposed, understand that. What man would be willing to admit that it had been his faithless behaviour which had driven his young wife to commit suicide? Nonetheless, a chill of misgiving crept through Kathryn, casting a dark cloud over the sunlit afternoon.

'Jamie,' Sebastian unexpectedly called, 'come back here. It's time for lunch.' It brought the conversation to an abrupt end, confirming Kathryn's suspicion that Sara's death had all been down to him and Cassie. But did he know about the letter? That was something she couldn't bring herself to ask.

Whether it was due to the fact that they were eating al fresco, or that Joyce's food was so delicious, between them they consumed everything that she'd packed. Eventually they leant back against the trunk of the tree, even Jamie — replete, satisfied, and drowsy in the hot afternoon sunshine. It wasn't too long before the little boy fell asleep, leaving Sebastian and Kathryn as good as alone together.

He sipped his wine and asked, 'Have you heard anything more from Matt?'

She was surprised; the last thing she'd expected was for him to mention the man he'd threatened to literally throw out of his house. 'Uh — n-no, as far as I know he's returned to Dubai.'

'Look, Kathryn, about what happened then — my behaviour . . . '

'Please, don't. I just want to say, I didn't invite his kisses. In fact, they were the last things I wanted.'

He looked at her for a long moment and then said, 'I realised that later. And then, for me to treat you the way I did — I'm sorry.'

'Forget it. I have.'

His look was an odd one then; it was made up of amusement mixed with hurt. She realised he thought she was alluding to his kiss.

She had her mouth open to put him

right about that when he said, 'I have to say he must be mad; clinically insane, in fact.'

'What do you mean?'

'To give you up.'

Kathryn looked at him, puzzled, confused. What did that mean? That he was attracted to her? 'We-ell, I don't know a-about th-that,' she managed to stammer.

'I do.'

Unnoticed by her, he'd moved closer. Their faces were only a couple of inches apart now. His breath feathered her skin, making her shiver with a deep yearning. She could smell his after-shave; it was madly intoxicating. In fact, it left her feeling as if she'd drunk a glass of the finest champagne. Her head spun; every nerve ending in her body tingled. She wanted him to kiss her, to hold her — so badly, even though she was pretty sure he was in love with someone else.

'Don't you realise how beautiful you are, Kathryn?' His voice was husky, low;

his eyes were full of — what? The admiration he was expressing? Passion? Or the intent to play yet more games?

Kathryn tried to give a light laugh of disbelief. It didn't work.

* * *

Instead, it erupted as a gasp. 'I wouldn't say that.'

He moved closer. His hair brushed her cheek. She shivered again. He was going to kiss her. 'Kathryn,' he said as his lips gently brushed her cheek, 'can I kiss you?'

Well that was a first, him asking if he could kiss her. She stared at him, not understanding. Was this some sort of new tactic? To get his way with her? Or could it be that she was wrong about him and Cassie? Her heart lurched at the mere possibility. Yet how could she be? She had that letter. It said it all — they were in love; wanted to marry. She stared at him, completely bemused. His lips parted as he looked back at her.

His eyes, once again, were mere slits; but even so, she could see the glint within them. She gasped.

He was laughing at her. Laughing at her naivety, for taking his game-playing seriously. Furious with him, as well as herself for believing he cared, she lurched upright — with the inevitable consequence. The wine slopped from her glass to land in a pool on her linen trousers. With fingers that shook, she rubbed at the spreading patch. Sadly, it only made it worse.

Sebastian laid his hand over hers, stilling her frantic movements. With his other one, he took the glass from her and set it on the grass next to his. 'Don't,' he softly admonished. 'It doesn't matter.' His gaze seared her, burning her skin. 'Kathryn, can I? Please?'

Kathryn felt her breath freeze in her throat.

'Haven't you guessed?'

Kathryn shook her head. 'G-guessed?'

'That I'm in love with you. That I fell for you the minute I saw you

— standing at my door, looking so adorably unsure of yourself.'

She stared at him, mesmerised by what he was saying.

He groaned as if in mortal agony. 'Don't — don't look at me like that, with those wonderful eyes that literally melt every bone in my body. Not if you aren't going to let me kiss you. Jamie knows how I feel, that's why he's been saying the things he has. My mother knows — I've had her on the phone practically every day, asking me if I've told you.' He gave an exasperated little snort. But all Kathryn could think was, his mother knew? So that must mean it hadn't been Cassie she'd been talking about. 'Everybody knows but you, apparently,' Sebastian went on ruefully, 'and I can't hide it any longer.' He slid an arm around her waist, gently drawing her in to him. 'I didn't want to rush things, scare you away — and I seemed to be in danger of doing just that every time I kissed you. But I can't go on without you — can't let you go, that's the truth of it. I've done everything I can think of to make you stay, bar locking you inside the house.' He gave a tentative smile. 'Please, please, don't leave us. Stay.'

She didn't know what to say; what to think. Other than — what about Cassie? 'I love you too, but — '

'But what?' he murmured, bending his head to kiss her.

She pulled back. She had to know the truth, no matter how much it hurt. It was time to have it all out in the open.

'Cassie — what about Cassie?'

18

Sebastian blinked at her. 'Cassie? What about her?'

'Have you been seeing her?'

He raised a quizzical eyebrow. 'Of course I've been seeing her. I help her with her financial affairs.'

She had to get it all absolutely clear, beyond any doubt. 'When I heard you and your mother talking one evening and she was urging you to tell someone how you felt about her — it wasn't Cassie that she meant? It was me?'

'Of course it was you. You've thought all this time that I was involved with Cassie?' He sounded genuinely astounded. 'No wonder you've been so standoffish, so furious whenever I kissed you. Why would you think that?'

She took a deep breath and plunged in. If he was lying it would end every one of her dreams, but she had to know the truth. 'I-I found a letter.' He stared at her, perplexed. 'A letter?'

'Yes, beneath the bureau in the hall. It was all scrunched up. I was trying to find a toy car that Jamie had rolled under there.'

He didn't speak; just waited with a gaze that was so intense, it was as if he were physically touching her.

'The letter was to Sara, from Cassie. Sara must have dropped it. I'm sorry; I should have given it to you.'

But he wasn't listening to her last few words; didn't seem bothered by the fact that she'd withheld the letter from him. All he asked was, 'Why would Cassie write to Sara?'

'She said that you and she were in love, and you were planning to leave Sara to marry her.'

'What? Oh my God.' He lifted his hands to cover his face. They were trembling.

'I have to ask — '

'No, no, no.' He was practically shouting, then realising that he'd wake

Jamie lowered his voice again. 'I was not in love with Cassie, or anyone else for that matter. I never have been — not till now.' He lowered his hands and stared at Kathryn, his anguish plain to see. 'It explains why Sara did what she did — Oh, jeez! She must have thought she'd lose all three of us.' His voice broke.

'I don't understand.'

'Then let me explain. As I've just said, Sara and I weren't right for each other, not even in the beginning. I don't know why we married. We would have split up but Sara fell pregnant almost at once with Jamie, so we decided to try and make it work. In vain, I regret to say. I make no excuses; I wasn't the best of husbands. I devoted myself to my work and almost neglected her — and Jamie, at times. She eventually and inevitably fell for someone else. She asked me for a divorce. I agreed, but told her I wasn't going to lose my son. I told her I'd fight her in the courts, if necessary, for custody of him. I promised that we'd share the care of him — but I wanted custody. From the things she'd said about him, I didn't trust her lover, Oliver, to look after Jamie properly. Anyway, to cut a long story short, just as she was on the point of leaving me, Oliver disappeared.' He snapped his fingers. 'Just like that. Went where? No one knew. She stayed with me, but descended into deep depression. In her mind she'd lost him, our marriage looked to be over, and if we parted she stood to lose her son as well.' He lapsed into silence and stared into the distance, his expression one of deep grief. 'It's my fault. As soon as I realised her state of mind, I should have taken her to a doctor and got her treatment, but I didn't. And then, getting the letter from Cassie that you've just described, well . . . it must have been what tipped her over the edge. She could see no future for herself, other than complete loneliness. The result — she went out, picked her moment and ran in front of a lorry.' He was shuddering, his expression bleakly grim. 'All my fault. I knew Cassie was fond of me; I just never realised how fond or to what lengths she'd go to get what she wanted . . . '

Kathryn's heart ached for him and for Sara. How unhappy she must have been; how desperate.

Kathryn couldn't help herself then. She put her arms around him and held him close. 'You couldn't have possibly known what she'd do. It's not your fault.'

They sat like that for some time and then Sebastian looked at her and groaned, 'I've never felt anything for Cassie other than friendship.'

'She obviously didn't see it that way. She wanted you, and saw writing the letter as a way of breaking you and Sara up. She couldn't have foreseen what her actions would lead to.'

'No, I don't think she did. She was terribly upset for a while after it happened. Her distress seemed excessive at the time, but I see now it was guilt. And then, with you on the scene, well, she obviously guessed how I feel about you, hence the spite. Thank God that's all she resorted to.' He stared at her, his expression one of anguish and deep uncertainty. 'You will stay with us, won't you? Marry me? I can't live without you. I love you — so much.'

'I love you too, so — yes, yes, I'll marry you. I've been so miserable.'

And he kissed her finally, a kiss that went on and on.

* * *

They went to see Kathryn's parents the next day, taking Jamie with them. Their news at first astonished Helen and Richard, but then made them smile broadly. Helen immediately took to Jamie, as he did to her.

'Will you be my granny?' he asked.

'If you'd like me to be,' Helen smilingly replied.

'I would,' he agreed.

Kathryn eventually took her mother

to one side and quietly asked, 'Have you had your results yet?'

'Yes, this morning. It's a benign cyst — easily removed. So all is well. I can get on with my life and help you plan your wedding.'

'Oh, thank heavens!' Kathryn cried. 'I've been so worried.'

Richard came and slipped his arm about his wife's waist. He'd obviously overheard their conversation. 'Great news, isn't it? As Helen says, we can get back to normal.' His expression darkened. 'At least, we could if the riddle of the thefts from work could be resolved.' He turned to look at Sebastian. 'I hear the police are no nearer to finding out who it is.'

'No,' Sebastian said, 'but they seem to have removed you from their list of suspects.'

'Dad,' Kathryn whispered to him, 'can I have a word? Something's worrying me. It may be nothing, but then again it could be something.'

They excused themselves and went

into the kitchen, where she told him about seeing an identical pair of earrings to Jess's. 'They were priced at a hundred and twenty-five pounds. She told us that Fitz gave them to her, but you've seen him. He looks as if he hasn't got two pennies to rub together. Where would he have got that sort of money from? As much as I hate to accuse either him or Jess of being behind the thefts at Supreme Foods . . . ' She paused, hating what she was about to do. 'She does have access to your work keys — here, I mean. It would be an easy matter for her to borrow them. You leave them on a hook in the hall all weekend.'

'Yes.' Richard stared at her incredulously. 'You're right. And I probably wouldn't even notice they were gone if it was only for a short while.' He frowned then. 'Your mother's been concerned about some of the clothes and things that Jess has been coming home with too, although Jess always insists that Fitz had bought them. I hadn't linked any of it with the robberies, though, and I should have.' He smacked his hand against his forehead. 'How stupid I've been. My only excuse is that my mind was on your mother rather than the thefts. But what can I do? I can't accuse my own daughter — and it may not be her.'

'No, don't accuse her. As you say, it might not be her. Have a quiet word with her — ' The front door opened. ' — and here's your chance. I'll leave you to it. Unless you want me to stay?'

Richard shook his head, but his air of unutterable defeat and helplessness prompted Kathryn to say, 'I'll speak to her. You go back to Mum and the others. Keep everyone in the sitting room.'

Jess strode into the kitchen just as her father made his exit. 'Hi, Dad.' She swung back to her sister. 'What's up with him? And why are you here again?' She didn't wait for Kathryn's answer before asking, 'And isn't that Grant's car out front?'

'It is. We've come to give you our good news.'

Jess eyed her. 'What good news?'

'We're engaged to be married.'

'What?' Jess gave a burst of ironic laughter. 'Well, congratulations. I have to hand it to you, he's a real catch. Will he give me my job back, now that he's about to become one of the family?' When Kathryn didn't reply, she turned to go upstairs to her room, muttering, 'I'll take that as a no then, shall I?'

'Jess, before you go . . . ' Kathryn paused, nervous about what she was going to have to ask her sister. Jess could exhibit quite a temper at times.

'Now what?' Jess wearily asked.

'I'm going to ask you something and-and I want an honest answer.'

Jess stared at her, something that looked very like dread in her expression. Kathryn felt her spirit sink. 'Are you and-and Fitz behind the thefts at Supreme Foods?'

Jess didn't speak for a long, long moment, but then something completely unexpected happened. She literally threw herself at her sister, sobbing loudly, 'Oh God, Kathryn, I haven't known what to do.'

'What do you mean? Is it you?' A sensation of dread clawed at Kathryn. Oh God, had it been her sister? How was she going to tell Sebastian?

'No, of course not,' Jess indignantly retorted through her sobs, although they were easing. 'I wouldn't do something like that. It-it's Fitz. He took Dad's keys while he was here one weekend — stupidly, I'd told him where they were. Lord knows why. But I trusted him. He had copies cut before returning them again and he and his mate used them to get in overnight and steal the food. Nobody even noticed the keys were gone.'

'Did you know what he was planning?' Because if she did, all Kathryn could think was that that made her an accomplice.

'No. But I'd begun to wonder where he was getting the money from to buy me things — he isn't all that well-paid — and then I overheard him and his mate, Bob, talking. Bob drives one of the delivery vans, and he said something that made me suspicious. I asked Fitz about it and he admitted they'd been stealing for quite a while. He'd been adding extra amounts to the van loads — only small amounts to start with — and Bob would sell it on. But then, when nobody realised that it was someone in the packing and dispatch department who was responsible for the thefts, as they'd only been checking bags and things as people left, they began to increase the amounts. Just a little each time, but enough for him and Bob to make a bit more money out of. Then he said Bob had got even bigger ideas. He knows the owners of a pub and a restaurant and he's been supplying them on a regular basis with our ready-made meals. He and Fitz have been splitting the money they made between them. The owners agreed to take more, a lot more, if Fitz and Bob could get it — which, of course, had to be done at night — hence taking Dad's keys and having them copied. They simply let themselves in and filled the van. I didn't know anything about it till recently. You have to believe me.'

'Oh, Jess, why didn't you tell Dad at once — tell someone?'

'Because when I threatened to do just that, he said no one would believe me. They'd think it was me; even my father would think that. I mean the keys were in my house, so I could use them at any time. And if Fitz was questioned he'd say it was all my idea. I've been so scared. I didn't want to finish with him in case he told somebody it was me. And Mum's acting so strange, I couldn't talk to her. Dad's distracted, remote. I didn't dare tell you, what with you working for and living with Sebastian. And then, when Dad was arrested, I didn't know what to do. I didn't want to see Fitz arrested.' She began to cry again, even harder this time. 'Because he'd have blamed me, I know he would. I'm sorry; I've been such a coward.'

Kathryn held on tightly to her sister, her own expression one of grim dismay. But at least Jess hadn't been directly involved, just rather stupid. For she should have ignored Fitz's threats and told Richard. He would have believed her.

'Kathryn, what's going on?'

Kathryn swung around. It was Sebastian, standing in the doorway to the kitchen.

'Are you okay? Only I heard someone crying.'

Richard came up behind Sebastian. 'Sorry, love, I couldn't stop him.'

With that, Sebastian strode across to his fiancée and put an arm around her. 'What's happening? Tell me.'

Kathryn didn't speak; couldn't speak. How could she tell him? He'd be bound to think Jess was involved. But it was Jess who blurted, 'It was a friend of mine, Fitz — one of the packers at Supreme Foods — and one of the van drivers behind the thefts from work. I'm sorry, Dad.' She managed a watery smile at her father. 'Fitz stole your keys and had more cut, and — '

'Fitz,' Richard sighed, in palpable relief.

Jess nodded.

Sebastian was regarding Jess steadily. 'But you didn't take part?'

'God no. I didn't even know about it until afterwards.'

Richard didn't speak; couldn't speak by the look of him.

It was Sebastian who took control. 'Okay, I'll notify the police and tell them what's happened. I'll need Fitz's full name and also the name of the van driver.'

* * *

And that was that. Jess was cleared of any involvement, to her family's relief. Kathryn suspected Sebastian had had a hand in that. It made her love him all the more.

As for Sebastian and Kathryn, they married three months later. Jamie was ecstatic, and when the news was broken to him two months later that he was to have a baby brother or sister, his joy knew no bounds.

'We're a proper family now,' he told his new grandmother, Helen.

'Yes, you are, darling,' Helen replied, watching her daughter and her husband kissing each other.

'It was all my idea, you know,' Jamie proudly told her.

Helen chuckled and hugged the little boy to her. 'Maybe not quite all, sweetheart. I think your daddy and Kathryn might have had something to do with it.'

THE END